CINDERELLA WALTZ

A Play

By
DON NIGRO

SAMUEL FRENCH, INC.
45 WEST 25TH STREET   NEW YORK 10010
7623 SUNSET BOULEVARD HOLLYWOOD 90046
LONDON

IMPORTANT BILLING AND CREDIT REQUIREMENTS

All producers of CINDERELLA WALTZ *must* give credit to the Author of the Play in all programs distributed in connection with performances of the Play and in all instances in which the title of the Play appears for purposes of advertising, publicizing or otherwise exploiting the Play and/or a production. The name of the Author *must* also appear on a separate line, in which no other name appears, immediately following the title, and *must* appear in size of type not less than fifty percent the size of the title type.

CINDERELLA WALTZ was first produced in June and July, 1978, by the Indiana State University Summer Repertory Theatre in Terre Haute, Indiana, with the following cast:

Rosey Snow . . . . Debra Adams

Mr. Snow . . . . Peter Dee

Mrs. Snow . . . . Mary Kababik

Goneril . . . . Donna Harlan

Regan . . . . Chris Jansen

Prince Alf . . . . David Silberman

Troll . . . . Larry Zuber

Mother Magee . . . . Dorothy St. Vincent

Zed . . . . Jerry Walker

It was directed by Gary Stewart. Costume design by Jeffrey Wolz. Set design by Robert Sypitkowski.

THE VORTEX THEATER COMPANY
Robert Coles, Artistic Director

presents

CINDERELLA WALTZ

by DON NIGRO

Directed by **ROBERT CHAPEL**

Scenic Design	Lighting Design	Costume Design
MICHAEL DAUGHTRY	DEBORAH CONSTANTINE	MARIA DOMINGUEZ CHAPEL

Production Stage Manager
DEBORAH TORRES

Sound Engineering
BARRY HOLBEN

CAST

Rosey Snow	Kathryn Layng*
Mr. Snow	James Hosbein*
Mrs. Snow	Libby Colahan*
Goneril	Mary M. Stein*
Regan	Andrea Garfield*
Prince Alf	Jack Kenny*
Troll	Sam Samuels*
Mother Magee	Barbara Rosenblat
Zed	David Wheeler

Place: The yard before the Snow family hovel in the middle of a great forest on the outskirts of Cinderville

Time: Once upon a . . .

ACT I: Scene 1: A spring morning
Scene 2: The evening of the ball

ACT II: The morning after the ball

There will be one intermission

*These actors are members of Actors' Equity Association, appearing without benefit of contract or salary. The donation of their professional services is with permission of Actors' Equity Association.

CHARACTERS

ROSEY SNOW
MR. SNOW, her father
MRS. SNOW, her stepmother
GONERIL &
REGAN, her stepsisters
PRINCE ALF
TROLL, his servant
MOTHER MAGEE, a fairy godmother
ZED, the village idiot

SETTING

The yard before the Snow family hovel in the middle of a great forest on the outskirts of Cinderville. A porch, an abandoned hog trough, rustic things, a tree and a grave by a well.

The music is E. Waldteufel's 'Dolores Waltz.'

CINDERELLA WALTZ

ACT ONE
Scene One

A spring morning. ZED sleeps in the hog trough. The morning sounds of one hopeful rooster, then another, a third, chickens, a cow, more cows, sheep, a growing din of pigs, horses, crows, pigeons, an odd howler monkey, exotic bird calls, climaxed by the trumpeting of an elephant, then fading into the sound of MRS. SNOW bitching as ZED begins to stir.

MRS. SNOW. *(from inside the house)* Rosey Snow! Rosey SNOW! WHAT ABOUT THE WASH?

TROLL. *(from deep in the well, a small voice)* Help. I'm down the well. Help.

ROSEY. *(emerging from the house with two petunias)* I just want to put petunias on my mother's grave. *(ZED, unnoticed by ROSEY, has gone over to the well and stuck his head in.)*

MRS. SNOW. *(Bullying ROSEY out, followed by GONERIL and then REGAN, who is combing GONERIL's hair.)* You didn't wash my bloomers. And what about the knickers? And have you forgotten the suspenders? Wash the windows, wash the cat, wash the washing, wash the chickens, wash your father, wash, wash, wash.

ROSEY. I need to get some water from the well.

7

MRS. SNOW. Wash the well.

TROLL. *(from in the well)* Help. I'm down the well. Help.

MRS. SNOW. I'll wallop you. I'll whack you with the broom, girl.

ROSEY. I can't wash without water.

MRS. SNOW. Wash the water, wash the tree, wash the rocks, wash the cornfield, wash the horse, wash the tractor, wash the camel, what's the matter?

ROSEY. *(Pointing to ZED'S legs, which are protruding from the well.)* There's legs in the well.

MRS. SNOW. Wash the legs.

REGAN. We don't have a tractor.

GONERIL. Whose legs?

ROSEY. *(pointing)* Right there. Protruding.

MRS. SNOW. Watch your language.

ROSEY. From the well. Look.

MRS. SNOW. My God, there's LEGS in the well.

ZED. *(Righting himself, looking at them.)* Er. Uh. *(He points down the well.)* Trrrrrrrrrrrrrr----

MRS. SNOW. GAKKKKKK. THE VILLAGE IDIOT. GET AWAY.

REGAN. IT'S THE VILLAGE IDIOT.

GONERIL. I can see that.

MRS. SNOW. What are you doing in that well? Shame on you. Go do it behind the barn. Get. Idiot.

ROSEY. Maybe he's friendly.

ZED. *(Moving towards ROSEY.)* ERRRRRK. UKKKKKK.

ROSEY. Then again, maybe not. *(He reaches a hand in her direction.)* EEEEEEEEEK. GET AWAY.

TROLL. Help. I'm down the well.

ZED. *(Pointing at the well.)* ERRRRRKKKKK. UKKKK KKKKK.

GONERIL. Did you hear something?

REGAN. I think he said, Errrrrrk, Ukkkkkkkkk.

GONERIL. No, not him.

(MR. SNOW sticks his head out the window of the house.)

MR. SNOW. Where's my pants? I've lost my pants. I can't find my pants.

MRS. SNOW. *(To ROSEY.)* And wash your father's pants. And wash his cumberbun. And his weskit and his dickey.

ROSEY. I washed his weskit and his dickey.

MRS. SNOW. What are we ever going to DO with you, Rosey Snow?

ROSEY. Probably ruin my life.

MR. SNOW. Where's my pants?

MRS. SNOW. Look under the cat.

ROSEY. They're not under the cat.

MR. SNOW. I looked under the cat.

MRS. SNOW. Well, look again, there's a lotta room under the cat. I bet your rotten daughter Rosey went and ate them. Rosey, wash the cat.

ROSEY. I just washed the cat.

MRS. SNOW. Wash it again.

ROSEY. You can only wash the cat so many times. The fur's starting to rub off.

MR. SNOW. Maybe it's under the bird. *(He pops back into the house.)*

MRS. SNOW. *(Noticing that ZED is still there.)* I thought I told you to GET.

ZED. Errrrrk. Ukkkkk.

MRS. SNOW. *(Beating him with the broom.)* FILTHY IDIOT. HOMICIDAL PERVERT. Go hang around in the village, lick little girls, kiss goats, just GET AWAY FROM ME. Good for nothing at all. Just like Rosey.

ROSEY. I'm good for something. I wash the cat.

MRS. SNOW. WELL, GET TO WORK THEN.

ROSEY. I just wanted to put these petunias on my mother's grave first.

MRS. SNOW. Oh, PISH in your petunias. Pardon my French.

GONERIL. She's just no good, Mother.

ROSEY. I am too good. I'm very good. I'm just unfortunate. And I've got these petunias.

REGAN. *(Combing GONERIL'S hair.)* She's partly good and partly not. Hold still, Goneril.

GONERIL. Don't yank.

REGAN. Then HOLD STILL. Criminetly.

MRS. SNOW. Rosey Snow is a disgrace and a disaster.

REGAN. She's partly a disgrace, and partly a disaster. Where's the curling iron?

GONERIL. Rosey stole it. She stole the curling iron.

ROSEY. I didn't steal it. Father sat on it. Why's everybody always picking on me?

MRS. SNOW. *(Noticing ZED again.)* Are you still here? Smutty old dishrag. GET. *(She beats him with the broom until he gives up and runs off.)* AND DON'T COME BACK TILL YOU WARSH YOUR NECK.

REGAN. Maybe a dwarf stole it.

ROSEY. It wasn't a dwarf.

REGAN. I saw a curly dwarf yesterday.

MRS. SNOW. There's too many of them damn dwarfs around here. I don't like it.

ROSEY. *(Dropping the bucket in the well.)* Don't talk bad about dwarfs. I like dwarfs.

GONERIL. It's like you to like dwarfs.

TROLL. *(from the well)* Ouch. I'm hit. I'm hit. *(ROSEY looks down the well.)*

MRS. SNOW. I don't like gnomes, neither. Always lookin' up yer dress.

GONERIL. You're a bigot, Mother.

MRS. SNOW. I'm not a bigot. I love dwarfs. I worship dwarfs. I go to church and pray for dwarfs. There's just too many of them runnin' loose around here. Every morning there's six or seven of 'em comin' down the road with pick axes whistlin' and singin' and screamin'. Scares me half out of my pants. A decent woman ain't safe.

(MR. SNOW appears on the porch, in long underwear.)

MR. SNOW. Somebody stole my pants.

GONERIL. *(Pointing at ROSEY.)* She stole his pants.

REGAN. It might have been a dwarf.

MR. SNOW. What would a dwarf want with my pants?

MRS. SNOW. Who started all this damn talk about dwarfs, anyway?

TROLL. *(from the well)* I like dwarfs.

ROSEY. I think there's somebody in the well.

REGAN. I like dwarfs partly, and partly I don't care.

MR. SNOW. Where's my pants, Gertie?

MRS. SNOW. Try the bread box.

MR. SNOW. Bread box. Check. *(He goes back into the house.)*

TROLL. HELP! PULL ME UP! THERE'S SNAKES DOWN HERE.

REGAN. There's somebody in the well. *(She peers down into it with ROSEY.)*

TROLL. Take my hand. I'm a stranger in Cinderville. Hold on. *(ROSEY and REGAN help to pull TROLL up.)* That's right. Pull. Fell in, you see. Ever so kind of you. Urkkk. Ukkkkk. *(They finally succeed in dragging him out.)*

MRS. SNOW. Land sakes, there was a little man in the well. Is that sanitary? Why didn't you say something?

TROLL. Yes. Excuse me. Thank you.

ROSEY. Are you all right?

TROLL. No. Thank you. Goodness, what an experience.

REGAN. What were you doing down the well?

TROLL. Oh, drowning for a while. Then I clung to the side with my fingernails for nine or ten hours. No problem. I'm dry now. Seersucker. *(He knocks water out of his ear.)*

MRS. SNOW. What?

TROLL. My name is Troll. How do you do?

REGAN. We had a troll in the well.

TROLL. No, I'm not really a troll, per se. That's just my name. My father's name was Troll. We lived under a bridge. I'm not what you'd call a troll, qua troll. I'm a perfectly normal person. More or less.

MRS. SNOW. You don't look normal.

GONERIL. He looks like a troll.

REGAN. I think he's cute.

TROLL. Well, I'm not. A troll.

ROSEY. Of course you're not.

GONERIL. He smells like a troll.

ROSEY. No he doesn't.

REGAN. He smells like tuna fish.

ROSEY. You're embarrassing him. He's blushing.

TROLL. Actually, I'm a retainer. I'm retained by Prince Alfred. Of Fafrid.

MRS. SNOW. Fafrid?

TROLL. Alfred. I've been touring the countryside hither and yon and such, delivering invitations to the big ball, and I was tramping along looking at the sky, which is my wont from time to time, and humming in the evening, and I inadvertently fell down what turned out to be, alas, your well.

REGAN. He does look like a troll, doesn't he?

ROSEY. I'm Rosey Snow and this is my stepmother Mrs. Snow and my stepsisters Goneril and Regan, and my mother's buried over there in that grave by the well and that's why I have these petunias. And my father's inside getting his pants out of the bread box. Did you say you're having a ball?

TROLL. Not really. Prince Alfred is having a ball. I'm just tramping through the countryside hither and yon and such.

MRS. SNOW. And you came all the way out here just to invite US, how NICE.

TROLL. Uh, er, well, uh—

MRS. SNOW. That's very considerate of the Prince, isn't it, girls?

GONERIL. Mother—

REGAN. We're invited? Oh, WOW. Far OUT.

GONERIL. No, Regan, he doesn't mean—

REGAN. But that's wonderful. Isn't it WONDER-FUL?

ROSEY. Well, it's at least interesting. I mean, it's different.

MRS. SNOW. The Prince is so nice, sending his trusted container—

TROLL. Retainer.

MRS. SNOW. —out all this way past East Liverpool and Nanty Glo just to bring poor little US invitations! Not the Hickeys nor the Glucks nor the Dipples, just US. You may send the Prince our deepest condolences.

GONERIL. Mother, listen—

MRS. SNOW. Don't bother me, Goneril, I'm in a transport of infatuation. I'm sending the Prince my condolences.

GONERIL. Mother, can't you SEE? Are you BLIND? He wasn't bringing us tickets. He doesn't know us from Myrtle McTurtle. He just fell in the well.

MRS. SNOW. Nonsense. The Prince remembers me. I have a reputation from the days when I had my gentle-man callers, before my first husband ran off with the midwife.

GONERIL. Listen, Mr. Troll, you don't really mean to say you have tickets for us, do you? You just got lost, and stumbled into the well, isn't that right? You don't know us from Myrtle McTurtle, right?

TROLL. Well, er, uh—that is—let me check. I'm not sure. Let me take a peek in my pouch. Snow. Let's see.

Sleet. Slush. Snail. Snick. I may have lost your invitation down the well.

REGAN. Oh, Mr. Troll, it MUST be in there. I've never been to a ball. It sounds so exciting. I'd just DIE if it was a mistake. I'd just keel over and EXPIRE. *(Her lower lip is beginning to quiver. TROLL notices. He tries a weak smile, looking in a rather frantic, desperate way through the pouch.)*

TROLL. Oh, it's here somewhere. Bit mucky in this pouch now. Oh, dear. *(He pulls out a frog.)* Heh heh. Frog. *(They all look at him, unsmiling.)*

FROG. Brekek.

TROLL. Sorry. *(He throws the frog over his shoulder back in the well. Water splashes out.)* There we go. Splosh. Hehh hehhh. Well, you see, folks, uh, the truth is—

(From close by in the woods, behind TROLL, the sea cow bellow of a hunting horn, TROLL jumps, startled, and lands with one leg in REGAN'S arms.)

PRINCE. *(from off)* Ahoy. Tally ho. I say there. Troll? Troll, old boy? Are you there?

TROLL. Oh, no, there's the Prince. He's come looking for me. I knew this would happen. I'd best get back in the well. Excuse me. *(He tries to crawl back in the well. Exclamations of horror and dismay from everybody as they try to keep him from jumping back in.)*

EVERYBODY. No. Wait. Don't do that. It's wet down there. There's snakes. We like you. Think of your mother. Stop. *(etcetera)*

(The PRINCE appears with a very long rifle, a hunting horn, and

a few stray animal pelts.)

PRINCE. I say. There you are, Troll. Watch out there, you'll fall into the well, what?

TROLL. *(Caught, he leaps to attention, bellowing, frightening and nearly deafening everybody.)* PRINCE FAFRID OF ALFRED.

(The PRINCE, startled, drops his gun, butt first, and it goes off as it hits the ground, BANG.)

TROLL. ALFRED OF FAFRID. ALL RISE, HAIL.

(A duck falls from the sky. TROLL pulls out a small tooter horn and blows a fanfare, and with the other hand he throws a burst of confetti, which hits the PRINCE directly in the face. MR. SNOW comes out of the house, still in his underwear.)

MR. SNOW. There's a duck in the breadbox. No pants. Just a duck. *(Seeing the duck on the ground.)* There's another one. It's an epidemic. Oh, hello.

MRS. SNOW. Put your pants on, Delbert, we've got company.

MR. SNOW. *(to the PRINCE)* You wouldn't happen to have an extra pair of pants on you, would you?

PRINCE. Uh, well, I don't know, uh— *(He looks around vaguely.)*

MRS. SNOW. Try the fish tank.

MR. SNOW. Fish tank. Why not. Don't mind me. Ducks everyplace. Guns going off. I'm an old man. Who cares? *(He goes back in the house, muttering.)*

TROLL. I'm very sorry, your majesty.

PRINCE. At ease, Troll. And uh, whoever. I was more than a bit put out about you, Troll, you know. You didn't come home last night, old boy. Not like you, Troll. Bit of hanky panky, what? You old dog.

TROLL. *(sheepish)* Actually, I—

PRINCE. Came out after you, crack of dawn, thought I'd get in a few whacks with old Betsey— *(to the others)* — That's the gun—while I was at it. Got something, too, some sort of bird thing— *(He holds up a very strange carcass.)* —or fish thing, I'm not sure what, poor thing. Glad to see you're all right. You ARE all right, aren't you? You smell rather ripe. Here, take my things, all right? *(He gives TROLL the gun and several carcasses. TROLL has a terrible time with them.)*

MRS. SNOW. *(Closing in on the PRINCE, trying to curtsy and bow at the same time.)* We're deeply gratified, your courtship.

PRINCE. *(Backing away from MRS. SNOW.)* Oh, hello. Yes, well, what's the story, Troll? Hmmm? Speak up.

TROLL. Well, er, uh— *(Struggling with the gun and carcasses, he turns and inadvertently thwacks GONERIL on the rump with the gun barrel.)*

GONERIL. Uk.

TROLL. Oh, so sorry.

(He rubs GONERIL'S backside sympathetically, gets slapped very hard, falls back, tries to catch himself with the gun butt and brings it down on REGAN'S foot. The gun goes off again, BANG.)

REGAN. AHHHHHHHHHHHHHHHH.

(Another duck falls.)

TROLL. Oh, excuse me, I was just— *(He makes a gesture and hits MRS. SNOW in the face with the carcasses.)*

MRS. SNOW. Awk. Watch it, buster. *(She pushes him away and, taken aback, he falls with his nose between REGAN'S breasts.)*

TROLL. Oh, gadzook, you're soft. Nice. You've got soft—

PRINCE. Troll, what ARE you doing?

TROLL. *(scrambling up)* Well, er, I was taken aback, and, uh—

PRINCE. Come on, Troll, spit it out, man, are you all right or aren't you?

TROLL. Oh, I'm fine, sire. These people saved me from a fate as bad as near-death, almost. I fell down the well.

PRINCE. Looking up and humming again, were you?

TROLL. I'm afraid so, sire. I can't seem to help myself.

PRINCE. You'll never change, Troll, will you? Oh, well, thanks so much, folks. Lots of pretty women in this group, yes?

MRS. SNOW. Thank you very deeply, your royal princeship. I'm Mrs. Snow, your very loyal subject. God bless the King. God help the Queen Mother. God save the whales.

PRINCE. *(Not too happy about MRS. SNOW.)* Yes. Quite. And are these your granddaughters?

MRS. SNOW. Daughters. They're my daughters. I was a child bride.

GONERIL. Four times.

MRS. SNOW. This is Goneril, my eldest, smart girl, ravishing, big mouth.

PRINCE. I'm genuinely ravished.

MRS. SNOW. And this is Regan, my youngest. Pert as a pickle, and almost as smart. As Goneril.

PRINCE. Right. Sorry about the foot.

REGAN. Oh, that's all right. I don't walk much.

PRINCE. And who's this here?

MRS. SNOW. Where?

PRINCE. *(Pointing at ROSEY.)* Here.

MRS. SNOW. Oh, that's not anybody.

PRINCE. It must be somebody. I mean, she's got teeth and hair and two of those and one of those and—

MRS. SNOW. That's just the cinderslut, forget her.

ROSEY. I'm her stepdaughter, Rosey Snow, and my mother's buried over there under that tree by the well.

PRINCE. So sorry. Charming creature you are, Rosey, charming. Bit underwashed, but, well, who isn't? Troll's a little peculiar, you know, but he's my, well, friend, more or less, and I do wish there was something I could do to repay all you good people.

TROLL. *(aside)* You might invite them to the ball.

PRINCE. What's that, Troll?

TROLL. *(Embarrassed, trying to whisper it aside.)* Ball.

PRINCE. What? speak up.

TROLL. Ball. BALL.

PRINCE. Would you like to go and lie down, Troll?

TROLL. BALL. THE BALL. DANCING. PALACE. WALTZES. BOSOMS. ETCETERA. YOU KNOW. BALLLL.

PRINCE. Calm down, Troll, you're going to hurt yourself.

TROLL. Sorry. Lost my head.

PRINCE. I say, I have an idea. Would you girls like to come down to a ball? It's rather embarrassing, actually, but my father, the king, bless his heart, a merry old soul, and all that, if you like sadistic fat men with satyriasis, anyway, he and the queen, my mother, sweet woman, nose runs all the time, they've got this idea that it's time I ought to get married, you know, and I wasn't much keen on the idea myself, if you want to know the truth—am I boring you? I'm boring myself. Happens all the time. Pay attention, Troll. So, mother got this idea for a great awful BALL, you see, isn't that clever? Clever woman, my mother, bit of a squint she's got, but clever, sometimes, alternate Thursdays, in any case she thought we might as well invite all the eligible, well, you know, MAIDEN types, and that sort of thing, and a few buxom wench types from the countryside for variety, minor gentry and whatnot, and, this is an awfully long story, isn't it? What point was I trying to make, Troll?

TROLL. You're going to marry the fairest girl at the ball.

PRINCE. Well, why didn't you say so?

MRS. SNOW. AHA! AHA! AHA! OHO! AHA!

PRINCE. Is this woman choking?

MRS. SNOW. AHA!

PRINCE. I suppose that means they want tickets, yes? Have you got tickets for them Troll?

TROLL. We have some for the Snick sisters.

PRINCE. Snook?

TROLL. Snick.

PRINCE. Are these women the Snick sisters?

TROLL. Not exactly.

PRINCE. Come on, Troll, I've had a rough day. Either they ARE the Snick sisters or they're NOT the Snick sisters, isn't that right? Didn't that woman tell us their name is Snog?

MRS. SNOW. Snow.

TROLL. They're close, alphabetically.

GONERIL. I knew it. I just knew it. There's no tickets for us. They hate us. We're nobody.

PRINCE. No you're not. You have very nice—

GONERIL. They're rich and famous and we're just DIRT. *(REGAN bursts into tears.)*

PRINCE. Oh, I wouldn't go that far. We're all dirt to some extent. I mean, you're quite a pretty girl, you know. So's your sister. So's—uh— *(Indicating ROSEY.)* —what's her name here. So's— *(He looks at MRS. SNOW.)* — well—

GONERIL. We're SCUM. We're FILTH. WE'RE SLUDGE. *(REGAN is sobbing.)* WILL YOU STOP THAT? *(GONERIL starts to sniffle. ROSEY is crying. MRS. SNOW bawls. The PRINCE looks at TROLL. TROLL looks at the PRINCE. TROLL begins to cry.)*

PRINCE. Oh, my. I knew this was going to be a bad day when Mother's glass eye fell in the oatmeal. I said to myself, Alf, this bodes no good. *(TROLL blows his nose loudly and cries on the PRINCE'S shoulder.)*

TROLL. I never WAS any good. I'm just no good.

PRINCE. Listen here, Troll, get a hold of yourself, man, there's peasants watching. I don't think there ARE any

Snick sisters. The Snick sisters must be a hundred and twelve if they're a day. What the devil are we inviting hundred and twelve year old virgins named Snick for, anyway? After all, Troll, really, what were you thinking of? Give these people their tickets. I remember Mother telling you distinctly to invite the Snopes.

TROLL. Snows.

PRINCE. There, see? You DO remember. I'm certain that Snick is a misprint for Snow, and I'm shocked, SHOCKED, do you hear, that you didn't realize that to begin with. Anyway, the Snick sisters are dead. We went to the funeral. You sang songs and played the accordion.

TROLL. Mouth organ.

PRINCE. Right. Give them the tickets, go on. *(Exclamations of delight and relief from the SNOWS.)*

SNOWS. Thank God. Hooray. Far out. Bless you. Big deal. Praise God. So what? Thank you, thank you, thank you. *(Etcetera. GONERIL tends toward the negative.)*

TROLL. Yes, sire. My mistake. Here you go, ladies. *(He gives the tickets to ROSEY.)*

ROSEY. This is remarkable. We have tickets. Something is actually happening to me. This is extraordinary. I'm impressed.

PRINCE. I'm glad we settled THAT. That's a load off my mind, I can tell you. Is everybody done crying?

REGAN. *(immediately bright)* I'm done. Are you done, Goneril?

GONERIL. Drop dead.

PRINCE. Yes. Charming.

REGAN. Oh, don't mind Goneril, she's real nice, mostly.

GONERIL. Regan—

REGAN. I remember one time when she was nine and I was eight and Rosey was in the barn, I got stung on the big toe by a mud wasp and Goneril sucked out the poison.

GONERIL. Regan—

REGAN. Even Mother was almost normal until she fell off the hay wagon and landed on her head. That was sad.

GONERIL. Regan, the Prince doesn't want to hear about Mother falling on her head.

MRS. SNOW. I'm perfectly normal.

PRINCE. Well, Troll, let's be off, what?

MRS. SNOW. I'm normal.

PRINCE. Things to do, you see, don't you know? Thanks so much.

ROSEY. I hope this isn't a trick. Could this be a trick?

MRS. SNOW. I only just fell off a little hay wagon on my head.

PRINCE. Prince business awaits. Say goodbye, Troll.

MRS. SNOW. It was only a ten or twelve foot drop.

PRINCE. Ta ta, cheerio, see you at the ball, what?

ROSEY. *(to TROLL)* This isn't a trick, is it?

TROLL. Probably.

PRINCE. Oh, by the by, watch out, I hear there's a homicidal idiot on the loose, best bolt the chicken coop, bites the heads off, poor devil. Bye bye.

REGAN. Goodbye! See you at the palace!

MRS. SNOW. Rosey's abnormal. Not me.

ROSEY. Could this be a real adventure?

PRINCE. These Snicks ARE lovely people, aren't they, Troll? *(TROLL is still dropping things and picking them up as they go out. REGAN helps, bringing him the two fallen ducks.)* I had a terrible time finding you, I really did. I mean, when I call your name, great hordes of TROLLS come. It's very disturbing. They come from miles around, and it's no fun explaining to an anxious lot of trolls that you don't really want them after you've clearly called them, what? I mean, really— *(The PRINCE and TROLL are finally gone.)*

REGAN. We're going to the BALL! We're going to the BALL!

GONERIL. It's going to be a disaster.

ROSEY. Is this the call to action? The shout from another room? Does romance beckon? Am I about to live through an archetypal folk motif?

MRS. SNOW. Rosey, you blockhead, why didn't you invite them in the house for lime-ade and macaroons?

ROSEY. I didn't imagine they'd probably WANT—

MRS. SNOW. Why can't you think of these things?

GONERIL. Why didn't YOU, Mother?

MRS. SNOW. Give me them tickets. *(She snatches the tickets from ROSEY.)*

REGAN. Those were real palace-type people. Rich people, Goneril. Real RICH people. Rich people are so handsome, and different, and handsome, and rich. Oh, I'm in LOVE and we're going to the BALL! I'm so excited.

ROSEY. I'm apprehensive.

GONERIL. I wish I was dead.

MRS. SNOW. Oh, there's so much to do. I just love life. I just love it.

ROSEY. How many tickets did he leave?

MRS. SNOW. Let's see. There's three tickets. Just enough. One for Regan. *(She give REGAN a ticket.)*

REGAN. Thank you, Mother.

MRS. SNOW. And one for Goneril. Take it, Goneril, or I'll jam it in your ear.

GONERIL. *(taking it)* Thank you, Mother. *(ROSEY holds out her hand expectantly.)*

MRS. SNOW. And one for ME. Now, what should I wear?

ROSEY. What about me?

MRS. SNOW. What ABOUT you?

ROSEY. What about MY ticket?

MRS. SNOW. The man only left three tickets. It's clear he wouldn't want to leave one for some smelly little cinderslut. After all, this man is a Prince.

GONERIL. Maybe he meant to leave YOU out, Mother.

MRS. SNOW. ME? LEAVE ME OUT?

REGAN. Well, you're already married, and you're, you know, older, and—

MRS. SNOW. You watch you step, Regan. That's pretty thin ice you're walking on. Stick your foot through and I'll bite it off. Sorry, Rosey, but that's what you get for going around in rags all day and reading the encyclopedia. What a mess you are. Anyway, you don't really want to go, do you?

ROSEY. Yes, I want to go. Of course I want to go. I've been dreaming about this all my life. What else have I got to think about? Washing the tractor?

MRS. SNOW. You don't even know how to dance, do you? And you haven't got a thing to wear. We, on the other hand, have closets full of nice dresses, don't we, girls?

REGAN. Maybe we could—

MRS. SNOW. Shut up, Regan. A dress won't help her if she has no ticket. And a ticket won't help her if she has no dress. And neither one will help her if she can't dance. So there we have it. It's God's plan. Let's go pick dresses, girls. Rosey, wash the pig, wash the buggy, wash the soap.

REGAN. I'm real sorry, Rosey.

GONERIL. Life is unfair.

MRS. SNOW. Come on and get in the house. My stars, what a couple of deadbeats. *(She bullies GONERIL and REGAN into the house, whining and complaining. ROSEY is left alone.)*

ROSEY. I think I've stumbled into a fairy tale. First the extraordinary opportunity, then the sudden obstacle. I read all about it in the encyclopedia. Do I see a pattern forming here? Is this an archetypal situation? Are my petunias drooping? Is this a typical fairy tale motif? And, if so, which one? And what should I do about it? I could put these petunias on my mother's grave. *(She goes over and does this.)* Oh, Mother, why are you dead? You're always dead when I need you. Oh, drat, stupid world. *(She sits down by the well.)* As I see it, I have two choices. I can kill myself, or I can do the washing and forget about it. But I CAN'T forget about it, and I don't want to kill myself, and I'm getting awfully sick of doing the damn washing. I want to go to the ball. Maybe I could just sigh and look glum for a while.

(She sighs and looks glum. ZED sticks his head out from behind a tree. MR. SNOW appears from the house, still without pants. ZED quickly disappears.)

MR. SNOW. They're not in the pickle barrel, not in the flour barrel, they're not in the wheel barrow, I looked in the chicken coop. I'm wasting my youth. What are you doing there, Rosey?

ROSEY. Thinking about my destiny.

MR. SNOW. Your what?

ROSEY. I'm fine.

MR. SNOW. I'm sure you're fine, but you're also sighing and looking glum. Is that normal? Are you sick? Did the horse die?

ROSEY. I guess I'm just being silly.

MR. SNOW. You be careful with that, Rosey. Your step-mother's been silly ever since she fell on her head, and I've just about lost hope it's ever going to pass. Silly is a very dangerous thing. Once it gets you, you're lost. Look at ME, for instance. Forty years in the cinder mines, and I don't even know exactly what a cinder is, or what it's good for, or why anybody cares, and I can't find my pants. I've caught the silly from your stepmother. I expect it's incurable. I was a serious man once. Those days will never come again. Never, never, never. Who was them strange folk comin' out from the well and such?

ROSEY. A troll from the well. A prince from the woods. And the village idiot from the hog trough, I think.

MR. SNOW. *(Shaking his head.)* This country's sure going to hell. You seen my pants?

ROSEY. Where did you take them off?

MR. SNOW. In the closet. I always take my pants off in the closet, Rosey, because your stepmother laughs at me when I take them off in front of her. Laughs and giggles. What a silly woman.

ROSEY. Maybe they're still in the closet.

MR. SNOW. I try to avoid the obvious places. Better look, though. If you're late at the cinder mines, the foreman eats your nose. Bites it right off. That's life. You're not going to sigh and look glum again, are you?

ROSEY. I'm all right.

MR. SNOW. I know you are. You've got a real nice body. I think about it all the time.

ROSEY. Goodbye, Father.

MR. SNOW. I'd best check the closet. You watch out for them sillies, now. Also the village idiot. Homicidal geek, that's what I hear. Listen, Rosey, could I maybe just put my hand on your—

ROSEY. FATHER.

MR. SNOW. Just kidding.

(He goes back into the house. ROSEY begins to sniffle. ZED sticks his head out from behind the tree and takes a few steps towards her, sneaky and ominous. When she speaks, he freezes.)

ROSEY. *(Washing the well disconsolately.)* STUPID BALL. I need you, Mother, and you're in the ground with the worms, turning into mulch. All my life I've been dreaming about going to the Fafrid palace and drinking plum punch and nobhobbing with the laids and lordies and being pretty and rich and clean and not having to dump out the chamber pots in the morning.

(The stage is darkening and is presently bathed in swirling lights, with confused faint people and waltz noises, Strauss, 'Vienna Blood.' ZED is moving gradually closer as she speaks, one hideous clawlike hand outstretched. Eerie and frightening.)

ROSEY. Oh, Mother, you were so pretty and clean. You wouldn't have taken my ticket. You used to tell me stories about princes and balls and kissing and things and you said I'd always be your little girly and I was special. Oh, it'd be so elegant, with everybody in pink and lavender all twirling around like tops and the floor so waxed and shiney like Mr. Macgregor's head. I'd make my entrance down a thousand and six step staircase like Natasha in *War and Peace* and we could dance waltzes and waltzes. The Prince is so handsome and funny and cute and everybody's twirling in circles like driblets on ice cubes and the colors go round and round like the world and we're all smiling and not getting dizzy or throwing up like Regan did on the whirlagig, and I'm getting swirled by the waist from lord to earl to viscount to duke to duchess till the Prince gets hold and won't let go, and we dance and dance in a little worldlike music box and the people dance and turn and the lights are turning so and the waltz is me and I just go on and on—

(ZED'S clawlike hand is just about to touch her neck when a great bellowing Tugboat Annie voice comes roaring out from the well. He jumps and runs for cover, still unseen by ROSEY, and the lights and noises go away.)

MOTHER MAGEE. *(from in the well)* YOOOOOOO

HHHHHOOOOOOOOOOOOOOOOO. OHO. HARK.

ROSEY. *(still half in the dream)* What?

MOTHER MAGEE. I say, HARK. HARK.

ROSEY. I beg your pardon?

MOTHER MAGEE. GIMME A HAND, DEARIE, I'M DOWN THE FRIGGING WELL.

ROSEY. Again?

MOTHER MAGEE. Again? Was I here before?

ROSEY. *(reaching into the well)* If this is another troll—

MOTHER MAGEE. Troll? Where? Help! Trolls! Where? *(ROSEY pulls MOTHER MAGEE up out of the well with some difficulty.)* Help. Trolls. Urgh. Arb. Lek. Ooooo. There. Oops.

(MOTHER MAGEE lands on her head and collapses in a heap outside the well, revealing garishly flowered bloomers.)

MOTHER MAGEE. My, my. Lordy, lordy. Goshnfishes.

ROSEY. Did you fall in the well, too?

MOTHER MAGEE. I don't think so. Did you?

ROSEY. Who are you?

MOTHER MAGEE. Rosey Snow?

ROSEY. No, I'M Rosey Snow.

MOTHER MAGEE. Good. Now, who am I?

ROSEY. I don't know. A troll?

MOTHER MAGEE. Thanks a lot, sweetie. I'm Mother Magee. Some name, huh? I'm a fairy godmother. Yours. It's true. I swear. Big surprise, right?

ROSEY. Really? You?

MOTHER MAGEE. What's the matter with me?

ROSEY. Well, nothing, exactly, I just thought—

MOTHER MAGEE. Who'd you expect? Tinker Bell?

ROSEY. Well, no, but—

MOTHER MAGEE. What do you need, kid? Piano lessons? A horse? I have Shetland ponies. How about a sucker? Tongue sandwich? Egg salad? Scuse me, honey, I've had a grim day. *(She takes out a flask and drinks.)* Guy named Rumplestiltzkin ate my dog. It was horrible.

ROSEY. Could you get me a ticket to Prince Alfred's ball?

MOTHER MAGEE. Just happen to have one right here. *(She immediately produces a ticket from her bosom and gives it to ROSEY.)* Now, if that's all—

ROSEY. This is a ticket to Switzerland.

MOTHER MAGEE. Oh. That's mine. Unless you'd rather go to Switzerland. I hear it's nice this time of year. Cheese. Clocks. Chocolate. Banks. Little blond guys in shorts. Yodeling.

ROSEY. No, I think I want to go to the ball.

MOTHER MAGEE. Suit yourself. Try this one. *(She produces another ticket.)*

ROSEY. Oh, thank you. It's got my name on it and everything. Rosey Snick. How'd you do that?

MOTHER MAGEE. Who knows? Well, I'm off to Venezuela.

ROSEY. Switzerland.

MOTHER MAGEE. Whatever. That all you want?

ROSEY. I don't have a dress.

MOTHER MAGEE. Here, you can have mine. *(She begins taking off her dress.)*

ROSEY. No, I don't want YOUR dress.

MOTHER MAGEE. I don't blame you. Neither do I. Been

trying to get rid of this damn thing for years. I'd just as soon run around naked, wouldn't you?

ROSEY. I don't ususally run around naked.

MOTHER MAGEE. Wouldn't hurt you any. Good way to make friends. Try this one. *(She reaches into the well and pulls out a box with a ribbon tied around it.)* I think it's your size. Wouldn't swear to it. Can't get good elfs any more. Made it from a cabbage leaf. Might pinch a bit up front. Gotta suffer if you want to be gorgeous. Believe me, I know.

ROSEY. *(Peeking into the box.)* Oh, it's lovely. It's moving.

MOTHER MAGEE. *(Reaching into the box and pulling out the frog.)* Frog. Got to watch that.

FROG. Brekkek.

MOTHER MAGEE. Ahhhh, shadddupp. *(She throws the frog casually over her shoulder and into the well. Water splashes up.)* Now, if you want slippers, here's a gift certificate from Mr. Glass the shoemaker's custom deluxe shoe shop and lawn mower repair. You get real nice ones, and a free shoe horn. I gotta run. Bye.

ROSEY. Wait. I haven't got any way to get to the ball.

MOTHER MAGEE. Take a horse cart. That's what I do.

ROSEY. I can't take a horse cart to the ball.

MOTHER MAGEE. Oh, all right. Go around the back of the house about six-thirty on the night of the ball and you'll find a pumpkin and some white mice, a rat and a couple of iguanas. Eat them for supper. Har har har. Just a joke. Say the magic word and they'll turn into a coach and horses and a driver and some footmen with long slithery tongues.

ROSEY. What's the magic word?

MOTHER MAGEE. Doorknob. No, ringworm. Sog waddle. No, it's, uh, NOVOTNY. That's it. Novotny. Say it.

ROSEY. Novotny.

MOTHER MAGEE. More feeling. Use your diaphragm. NOVOTNY.

ROSEY. NOVOTNY.

ROSEY & MOTHER MAGEE. NOVOTNY. NOVOTNY. NOVOTNY.

MOTHER MAGEE. Just remember, it rhymes with YA GOT ME. And don't say kolodny because it isn't kolodny, it's novotny. So many girls kolodny when they mean novotny and vice versa, and I wanta tell ya, you say the wrong magic word and you can end up with a squid in your lap. And you better be home by midnight, or the coach will turn into a pomegranate and the mice and rats into pitted prunes and you'll turn into a cabbage. Gotta watch them cabbage worms. Eat right up your leg. All right? Satisfied?

ROSEY. Oh, it's perfect, except—

MOTHER MAGEE. You bet your life it's perfect. Dearie, I'd love to stay and chew the fat with you, but I've really got to fly. Bingo this afternoon. Bye bye now. *(She starts clambering back into the well.)*

ROSEY. WAIT. WAIT. I can't dance. How can I go to the ball if I can't dance?

MOTHER MAGEE. Well, I'll tell ya— *(Reaching up her finger to make a point, she loses her balance and falls head first into the well.)* AAAAAAAAHHHHHHHHHHHHHHHHHHH.

(A splash and a great deal of water slops out, ROSEY just managing to avoid it, then hurrying back to call down the well.)

ROSEY. Come back. Come back. *(She sits down in despair.)* I should have gone to Switzerland. I don't see a happy ending here. Management is definitely winning. My destiny is to stay here forever and wash my father. Oh, drat. Double drab drat. Stupid world.

(She sobs. ZED appears again from behind the tree, moves closer, hesitates, moves towards her again, stops, hesitates, tries to speak.)

ZED. Errrrrrr—

ROSEY. *(very testy)* What?

ZED. Errrrrrrrrrrrrrrr—

ROSEY. *(Turning around and seeing him.)* AHHHH-HHHHHHHH. GET AWAY.

ZED. Errrrrrr, uhhhhh, ddddddddddddddddd—

ROSEY. HELP. ASSAULT. MOTHER. HELP. Oh, what a rotten day. HELP. FIRE. AHHHHHHHH-HHHHHH. *(She runs into the house.)*

ZED. *(looking after her)* Errrrrrgggggggg? ARRRRRRR-GGGGGGGGGGGGGGGGGGGG. *(Storming around, having a frustration fit, stomping and swinging his arms.)* RRRRR-RRRRGGGGGGGGGGGGGGGGGGGG. ARRRGGGGGG. RRRRRGGGG. YARRRRRRGGGGGG. AHHHHHHHHH.

(He falls over, breathing heavily. Sits up, glum. Pulls out a small mechanism, like the insides of a music box. Winds it up. It plays the little Waldteufel waltz. He sets it down and listens to it glumly. From somewhere, the long sad moo of a lovelorn cow. Lights fade and out.)

Scene Two

*The evening of the ball. Chatter from inside the house. GONERIL
and REGAN emerge, in tacky and ratty old ball regalia,
trailed by ROSEY, still in rags, who is trying to finish sew-
ing the hem of REGAN'S dress. MRS. SNOW follows,
hideously dolled up.*

Mrs. Snow. Oh, the night of the BALL. The NIGHT of
the BALL. Glory, I'm excited like a coffee pot.

Goneril. Relax, Mother.

Mrs. Snow. I won't relax. I'm too young to relax. Oh, I
feel like a summer chicken, I just want to peck my
feathers and cluck. Isn't life wonderful? Aren't I wonderful? Don't brood, Goneril, some near-sighted man will
want you. Aren't you done yet, Rosey? You don't want
your sister to be late, do you? You want her to trip and
break her neck on a stump? No, spite, Rosey, spite's a sin.
Oh, I LOVE BALLS.

Regan. I'm ready. Let's go.

Mrs. Snow. Goneril, you didn't pluck your eyeballs.
Rosey, get the giant tweezers and pluck your sister's
eyeballs.

Goneril. Eye-BROWS, Mother.

Rosey. Yes, Ma'am. Just a minute.

Mrs. Snow. I want it NOW. Do you want your sister to
have fat disgusting eyeballs? Oh, durn, I forgot my mole.
My artificial mole. For my face. Knocks 'em dead. Where
did I put that? *(She goes back into the house.)*

REGAN. Mother, we'll be late. You've already GOT moles.

GONERIL. Let's go, Mother, and get this stupid thing over with.

REGAN. It's not stupid.

GONERIL. It's VERY stupid. We LOOK stupid. We ARE stupid. Everything is stupid. I think God invented you people on purpose just so you can make me look stupid.

REGAN. Oh, that's not true. You'd look stupid without us.

GONERIL. Don't start, Regan.

REGAN. *(sing-song)*
Kill-joy, kill-joy,
Party Pooper, Sad Sack.

GONERIL. I can't stand it. I just can't stand it. Why all this meaningless suffering and humiliation? Nothing but heartache, heartache, heartache. Can't you see this in its existential perspective? Those rich people are going to laugh big laughs at us. They're going to GUFFAW, Regan. Look at these dresses, and this awful makeup, and our hair, for God's sake. We look like a bunch of female impersonators. Nothing good is ever going to happen to us. We're doomed. DOOOOOMED.

REGAN. Are you unhappy, Goneril?

GONERIL. WHAT KIND OF FAMILY IS THIS? Daddy's always running around in his underwear and Mother's all gooney and you've got the brain of a stuffed animal and Rosey carries petunias and keeps her head in a bucket of Spic and Span all day, and I can't take it any longer. What kind of respectable rich person is going to look twice at a monster like me?

REGAN. I think Goneril's in love.

GONERIL. YOU PEOPLE MAKE ME VIOLENTLY NAUSEOUS.

REGAN. I don't care. I'm going to have a good time, no matter what, and if Mother doesn't like it, she can kiss my horse.

(MRS. SNOW returns with a large mole in the middle of her forehead.)

MRS. SNOW. There. Now, where's them tweezers?

REGAN. Forget the tweezers, Mother. I want to dance 'till the cows come home.

MRS. SNOW. Just don't wet your pants, Regan. If nobody cares about Goneril's revolting, ugly eyeballs, if nobody cares that Regan's going to trip on a stump and flatten her nose, all right. Ready?

REGAN. Yes, Mother.

GONERIL. Yes, Mother.

MRS. SNOW. Then here we go, ready or not. Delbert? Rosey, get your father out of the corn crib. Last time he fell asleep in there, a black snake tried to swallow his— DELBERT!

REGAN. He's not in the corn crib, Mother, he's in the little house beside it.

MRS. SNOW. He's in the hen house?

GONERIL. He's powdering his nose.

MRS. SNOW. In the hen house?

REGAN. No, Mother, in the— *(She whispers in her ear.)*

MRS. SNOW. Well, why can't you just come right out

and say shithouse? Delbert's in the shithouse.

REGAN. It's not genteel, Mother. We're all dressed up. We're going to see rich people.

MRS. SNOW. That's a good point, Regan. Pardon my French. What do rich people call it?

REGAN. They don't call it anything, Mother. They have servants.

MRS. SNOW. GET OUT OF THERE, DELBERT, AND COME SAY GOODBYE TO ALL THESE BEAUTIFUL WOMEN. I hope to Moses he didn't get stuck. Last time it left a circle on him, lasted a week, so red it glowed in the dark.

(MR. SNOW emerges from the house, half asleep, in socks and long underwear.)

MR. SNOW. Time for breakfast? Ovaltine? Crunchy stuff?

MRS. SNOW. No, you booby, we're off to the ball. Don't wait up. Rosey'll give you your Ovaltine and a good burp. I'll bet you want a nice big smooch, don't you?

MR. SNOW. *(flinching)* Smooch?

MRS. SNOW. Not in front of the children, you animal.

GONERIL. MOTHER, LET'S GO. GO. LET'S GO.

MRS. SNOW. All right. Kiss me quick. Just one. Smooch smooch. Control yourself. *(She offers her cheek. He smiles weakly and kisses it.)* That's enough. Fresh. *(She slaps him hard across the head.)* NOW. Let's go. What's the holdup? Oh, Rosey, how I envy you your pleasant night of mumbly peg by the chicken coop and squarshing fireflies by the sump hole. Wish WE could do that. It's hard work, nobhobbing with the great and the near great. The advantages of the homely and untalented wallflower are too seldom noted. Lucky you. Bye, now. Oh, and wash the woodwork, wash the birdcage, wash the bird, wash the clock, wash your feet— *(GONERIL and REGAN are dragging MRS. SNOW off.)*

REGAN. Goodbye, Rosey. Goodbye, Father.

GONERIL. Goodbye, Father. Goodbye, Rosey.

MRS. SNOW. Don't drag me, I can still walk, for corn sake, you want to dislocate my elbows?

ROSEY. *(waving)* Bye. Goodbye. Have a nice time. *(They are gone.)* Choke on the hors d'oeuvres, Mom.

MR. SNOW. Is it time for bed already?

ROSEY. Yes, Father, go to bed.

MR. SNOW. You want to undo this button, here? You look kinda peculiar, Rosey. You didn't want to go to that ball, did you?

ROSEY. I guess I'm not really a ball sort of person, Father. I'll just stay home and shuck corn or something.

MR. SNOW. Nice, sensible girl. Won't find nothin' special at no ball. Warm your toes by the fire, curl up in your socks, cuddle a quilt in a softy rocker, look at the fire and scratch an old pussy, drink hot marmelade and butterscotch, read old dirty stories in the twilight, listen to the clock burp. That's what I call fun. *(He yawns.)* I'm putting myself to sleep. Well, nighty night. Sweet dreams and such. You get to feelin' bad, you come in and see your old Pap, we'll pray and chirp like birds and tell old jokes and laugh at the cat.

ROSEY. I think I'll paint my toenails.

MR. SNOW. Yeah, well, whatever. Here, kitty. *(He goes into the house. ROSEY sits by the well.)*

ROSEY. Ohhhhhhhhhh. Rrrrrggggggg. Rrrrggggg. I'm feeling anxiety. God help me, I'm scared as a turtle and I can't dance. I've got rats and a pumpkin and lizards and a cabbage leaf and I can't dance. I'm distraught, Mother, and you're buried by the well and I can't dance. Damn silly thing to do, bury Mother by the well, we can taste her every Thursday or Friday, OH, Mother, I want to cry, I'm chicken and I don't know how to dance. I'M DISTRAUGHT. I'M DISTRAUGHT. Is this my destiny?

(ZED appears from behind the tree.)

ZED. ERRRRRRRRRRRRRRRRRR—
ROSEY. *(jumping and screaming)* AAAAAHHHHHHH.
ZED. *(Startled by her, also jumping and screaming.)* AAAAAAAAAAAHHHHHHHHHHHHHHHHHH.

ROSEY. What do you want? You keep away. I'm in a bad mood. Slimey old village idiot. Ikkkkkkkk.

ZED. *(Moving to cut her off from the house.)* Errrrrrrrp.

ROSEY. *(Scared and partially cornered, trying to act natural.)* I beg your pardon. I didn't mean to be rude. You startled me, is all.

ZED. *(waving his arms)* Errrrr-uhhhh—dddddddddd—
ROSEY. Would you like some garbage? There's some garbage around back. Do you want some? It's fresh.

ZED. NAAAAAAAAA.

ROSEY. Okay. Okay. No garbage. *(She moves back a bit as he moves closer. They begin to make a small circling pattern.)* My seventeen brothers and uncles are just out in the tool

shed. I'll call them and have them drag you out some
chickens if you like. You know. Buck-buck-bu-GAWK.

ZED. *(moving closer)* NAAAAAAAA.

ROSEY. *(Very alarmed, cut off from the house.)* Uh,
FATHER! I'm just calling my father. He never sleeps.
I'm sure he's wide awake. FATHER. Uh, BROTHERS?
UNCLES? Arnold? Butch? Clyde? Deke? Everett?
Frenchy? Grumpy? Harpo?

ZED. ERF. ERF.

ROSEY. *(nearly hysterical)* WHAT DO YOU MEAN, ERF
ERF?

ZED. DDDDDDDDDDDDDDDDDDDDDDDD.

ROSEY. *(frantic)* DDDDDDDDDDD? As in DEADD-
DDDDDD?

ZED. Dddddddddddaaaazzzzzzzzzzzzzzzz.

ROSEY. Get away. I've got a pitchfork in my bodice.

ZED. *(pointing to himself)* Zddddddddd. ZZDDDDDDDDD.

ROSEY. What?

ZED. *(pointing to her)* Rrrrrrrrrrrzzzzzzzzzzzyyyy.

ROSEY. Rrrrrrrrrzzy? Oh, Rosey? Me?

ZED. *(A breakthrough. Very excited.)* YA YA YA YA YA YA
YA YA YA YA YA.

ROSEY. *(terrified again)* AAAAAHHHHHHHHHH.
(She tries to hide in the hog trough.)

ZED. *(immediately quiet)* Nnnnnnnnnnn. Okay dokey.
Ssssssoft. Okay? Rrrrrzy?

ROSEY. *(Looking up cautiously like Kilroy from out of the hog
trough.)* You know my name, huh?

ZED. Rapunzel.

ROSEY. No, it's Rrrrrzy.

ZED. Nuh uh. Rapunzel. Miz.

ZED. *(Holding up four fingers.)* Thrid. Threeed. Tree. Grayyyyyyd.

ROSEY. Third grade? Miss Rapunzel?

ZED. *(excited again)* YAYAYAYAYAYAYAYAYAYAYA-YAYAYAYAYA.

ROSEY. *(Ducking back into the hog trough.)* Okay. Okay. Okay. *(Pause. ZED calms himself, says nothing, holding his mouth, watching the hog trough.)* You're not Miss Rapunzel. Miss Rapunzel was my third grade teacher. So what? How do you know that?

ZED. ZZZZZZZZZZZzzzzzzzzzzzzzzeddddddd. *(modestly)* Me.

ROSEY. *(Sticking her head up.)* Zed? *(He nods a lot, keeping quiet with some effort.)* You're ZED. *(He smiles and nods violently.)* I KNOW YOU. You used to make mud pies with me.

ZED. Ya. Yummmmmmmmmmmmmmmmmm.

ROSEY. Oh, Zed, what happened to you? Zed, you were a nice little boy. A little weird around the edges, maybe, but basically nice. Do you really eat birds whole and all that?

ZED. Naaaaaa. Listen. Dddddddazzzzzz.

ROSEY. What?

ZED. *(Forming the words with great difficulty.)* Ddddda-zzzzzzz. *(He makes little hopeful awkward circles with his hand.)* Ddddans?

ROSEY. Dance?

ZED. Ya. Ya.

ROSEY. What about it? You want to dance?

ZED. YAYAYAYAYAYAYAYAYA.

ROSEY. I need to go wash the goldfish.

ZED. *(blocking the way)* Naaaaa. Ddddanzzzzz. Hmmm?

ROSEY. I don't know how to dance.

ZED. Yowanta? Yowanta?

ROSEY. Yo-wan-ta?

ZED. You. Ta dans. Yes?

ROSEY. Ohhhhhhhh. I don't understand.

ZED. *(having a frustration fit)* URG. URG. URG. URG. URG. IDIOT. STUPID IDIOT. DORTY RATTEN RASELFRATSA. *(He is raging in a circle, beating his head against the well-bucket, tearing his hair, wild-eyed, sobbing.)* URG URG URG URG URG URG URG URG URG URG.

ROSEY. *(terrified again)* Mother? Father? Harpo? Help.

ZED. DDDDDDDDDAAAANNNNNNNSSSSS. GODAMNNNNNNNDANCE.

ROSEY. *(in tears)* I don't know what you want. I can't dance and I don't know what you want me to do and I can't go to the ball so stop picking on me and my twenty-six and a half brothers and uncles are in the bread box with the garbage and in just a minute I'll get them to cut off your head and all your private parts so just leave me alone.

ZED. *(Trying very hard to control himself. Grabbing her by the shoulders and trying to enunciate.)* Teeeeeeeeeeeeccchhhhh-OOOOOOOOOOOOOOOOOO.

ROSEY. Gesundheit.

ZED. No. Teachooooo. Me.

ROSEY. Tea chew?

ZED. *(Sitting down by the well in despair.)* Laslfratal. Erg erg. Hosenfoph.

ROSEY. Oh, don't say that. I wish you wouldn't cry.

You shouldn't do that. It makes my teeth hurt. You can have all the chickens and garbage you want. Even the canary. Maybe not the canary.

ZED. *(Twirling his hands around hopelessly.)* Idiot. Can't talk. Total idiot.

ROSEY. You're talking. Say it again, slowly.

ZED. Teeech. Yooooo. Tadanz.

ROSEY. Teach me to dance.

ZED. YAYAYAYAYAYAYAYAYAYAYAYA.

ROSEY. JUST DON'T DO THAT, ALL RIGHT? You can teach me how to dance? Really?

ZED. Me.

ROSEY. You know how to dance?

ZED. Me. Ya. Can.

ROSEY. You've been eavesdropping on us. Shame on you.

ZED. *(looking guilty)* Same on me. Wanna dans?

ROSEY. *(Looking at him, hesitating.)* I think I'd better go. My brothers—

ZED. Ya. Harpo. Okay.

ROSEY. You can really teach me how to dance?

ZED. Pretty funny, ya?

ROSEY. You're talking better than you were.

ZED. Gave up. Talk better when you don't try.

ROSEY. We don't have any music.

ZED. I got music. Here. *(He takes out the little wind-up thing and shows her.)*

ROSEY. That's music?

ZED. This is a thing. MAKES music. Watch. *(He winds it up carefully. It plays. He puts it on the ground.)*

ROSEY. Oh. That's amazing. That's really amazing.

ZED. Ya.

ROSEY. Did you find that somewhere?

ZED. Nup.

ROSEY. Steal it?

ZED. Made it.

ROSEY. Oh.

ZED. Wandda danns? Easy.

ROSEY. *(backing away)* You stay there.

ZED. Can't teach from here. Short arms.

ROSEY. Uh, well, you're, uh, dirty.

ZED. Ya.

ROSEY. I'm not going. I want to stay home, warm my toes by the cat, curl up in the rug, scratch the clock, drink my socks. What do I want with some old Prince, just because he's good-looking and charming and rich and funny and very clean—

ZED. Okay. I go. Bye bye. *(He picks up the music thing, which stops.)*

ROSEY. Is it hard? I mean, to dance?

ZED. Easy for you. You know how.

ROSEY. I don't know how.

ZED. Sure you do. Forgot you knew. Chicken. Buck-bu-GAWK.

ROSEY. I'm not chicken.

ZED. Bye bye.

ROSEY. Okay. Let's dance.

ZED. Okay dokey. *(He winds up the music thing. It plays. He puts it down, holds out his arms. She moves cautiously towards him. He puts one hand lightly on her waist, takes it back, wipes it on his pants, replaces it, takes her hand with the other.)*

ROSEY. *(Allowing him, but with some distaste.)* I can't do it.

ZED. You follow. Easy. They taught us in the third grade. Miss Rapunzel. You remember. Long hair. Easy. Two one three. Two one three. Waltz is magic. Old times, like. Riding a bicycle.

ROSEY. I never rode a bicycle.

ZED. You danced.

ROSEY. I rode a goat. I'm awful.

ZED. Learning is awful. Awful is good. Dance. *(She is improving considerably.)* See? You know how.

ROSEY. I do. I remember. I do know how. *(Very happy. They dance.)* I can dance. I can dance. I can dance.

ZED. *(very happy)* Ya. Ya. Two one three. Ya.

ROSEY. *(Stopping abruptly and walking away.)* No I can't.

ZED. You just did.

ROSEY. I'll forget. I'm no good under pressure.

ZED. Naw. You got a pumpkin, mice, all that stuff.

ROSEY. I don't belong at any ball. I don't want to be a mythological heroine. What can you do with a Prince? I'd be just as happy home milking the bull.

ZED. I doubt it. *(Pause. They look at each other.)*

ROSEY. I have to go, don't I?

ZED. Yup.

ROSEY. I'm scared.

ZED. Me too.

ROSEY. What are YOU scared of?

ZED. I dunno. Things. Idiot. Got no words. Scared is not a reason.

ROSEY. *(After a moment. Sigh.)* Yeah. I better get dressed. I'm really late. *(She rushes towards the house, stops, turns.)* Stay and tell me if I look all right?

ZED. Ya. *(She runs into the house. ZED looks at his fingers. He picks his nose, stops himself with the other hand, sits, stands. From the well, sudden druken song. He jumps.)*

MOTHER MAGEE. *(Singing, from in the well.)*
Who's that knockkkkkkkking at my door?
Who's that knockkkkkkkkking at my door?
Who's that knockkkkkkkkking at my door?
said the fair young maiiiiiiiiidennnnnn.
IT'S ONLY ME FROM ACROSS THE SEA
SAID BARACLE BILL THE SAILOR.
(struggling to get out) Urf. Ug. Help. Ug. Give me a hand, will you, sailor? A foot? Any old part you like. Help a poor old woman get out of the well. Thankee.

(ZED is helping her out with some difficulty. She is clutching a flask and laughing like a banshee.)

MOTHER MAGEE. Wheeeeeeeeeee.

ZED. *(straining)* Urg.

MOTHER MAGEE. Oho, bucky, no liberties there, watch it. *(They land in a tangled mess on the ground by the well.)* Ug. There. Well, hello. Village idiot, right? I know you. Cave in the seven acre wood? You make them little mechanical doodads, right? Ya?

ZED. Ya.

MOTHER MAGEE. Teach her how to dance yet? Don't look astonished, kid. I'm close to omniscient when my feet don't hurt. Want a drink? Wonder gin. Swear by it.

ZED. No thanks.

MOTHER MAGEE. Suit yourself. Must be rough, bein' an

idiot and all, huh? Takes all kinds. Ain't easy bein' a fairy godmother, either, believe me. I could tell you stories that would make your toes curl backwards. Nice kid, Rosey, huh?

ZED. Ya.

MOTHER MAGEE. Smart, too. Now, you take some of these fairy tale types, they're nice to look at, and all that, but DUMB—Jeee-zoooey. Had one last week, had a brain like a bird's egg. That girl put her dress on sideways and blew her nose on the table cloth, but she was pretty, and she got what she wanted. I expect Rosey will, too. In the cards. Nice Prince.

ZED. Ya.

MOTHER MAGEE. How long you been an idiot?

ZED. Off and on.

MOTHER MAGEE. Ya. Come on, have a snort of this stuff.

ZED. Naaaaaa.

MOTHER MAGEE. Lordy, here she comes.

(ROSEY comes out shyly, in her gown.)

ROSEY. Hi. Hello. *(They stare at her.)* What's the matter? Do I look that bad?

MOTHER MAGEE. My dear, you are a transfiguration. Ain't she a transfiguration, son?

ZED. Ya.

ROSEY. You don't think I look silly?

ZED. Naaaaaa.

ROSEY. What if I forget how to dance?

ZED. Naaaaaa.

MOTHER MAGEE. You better hurry up, sweetie. The ball's already started. Go on.

ROSEY. Oh, all right. All right, what the hell. Thank you. *(She gives MOTHER MAGEE a kiss on the cheek, approaches ZED with the same intention.)* And thank you. *(She thinks better of it, gives ZED a hearty handshake instead, and runs out.)*

MOTHER MAGEE. *(shouting after her)* You be careful with that pumpkin, now. Don't let those mice get reckless. They're WILD, I tell you, just WILD.

ROSEY. *(From off, behind the house.)* All right. *(They stand there, both rather saddened. MOTHER MAGEE takes another drink from her flask.)*

MOTHER MAGEE. I don't know why I never get to go to the ball. Lord knows, I deserve it. I've sent so many of these poor neglected stepdaughters off to marry the Prince, I begin to wonder sometimes why couldn't I just go off to that ball, get a Prince for myself? Not in the cards. Magic only works on other people. Some of us are fairy godpersons, some dwarfs, some village idiots, etcetera. How it is. Ya?

ZED. Ya.

MOTHER MAGEE. You wouldn't like to dance, would you? I do a mean fox trot.

ZED. No thanks.

ROSEY. *(from behind the house)* NOVOTNY. *(pause)* NOVOTNY. NOVOTNY. NOVOTNY. *(pause)* NO-VOTNY.

MOTHER MAGEE. There goes the old novotny. She's off. *(She looks at ZED.)* Have a drink.

ZED. Ya. *(He takes the flask and drinks.)*

MOTHER MAGEE. You keep it, son. Want some more? Take a spare. *(She produces another flask and gives it to him.)* Have another one. *(She keeps giving him more flasks as she speaks.)* I got a million of them. Well, I'm off to someplace or other. Anything I can do for ya before I go? Like me to turn you into an upper class twit and have you ride off on a horse with some peabrained girl of your own? Hmm? Like that?

ZED. No thanks.

MOTHER MAGEE. Just as well. Don't think I could. Once an idiot, always an idiot. They also serve who only stand and drool. Well, hang loose, dummy. *(She walks rather forlornly away from him, towards the well.)*

ZED. Hey.

MOTHER MAGEE. Yo?

ZED. You want to dance?

MOTHER MAGEE. Love to.

ZED. Ya.

(He sets down the flasks by the hog trough, winds up the music thing. It plays. He sets it on the ground. They dance. Lights fade and go out. End of Act One.)

ACT TWO

Scene Three

The morning after the ball. Morning sounds as before. ZED sleeps in the hog trough, clutching one of MOTHER MAGEE'S flasks. Empties litter the ground beside it. From off, the sound of dwarfs singing:

DWARFS. Heigh ho! Heigh ho!

(They whistle. ZED holds his ears and disappears into the hog trough as MRS. SNOW emerges from the house, a large ice pack on her head.)

MRS. SNOW. YOU STUPID DWARFS, WILL YOU JUST SHUT UP? STOP THAT GODDAMNED WHISTLING, YOU'RE DRIVING ME CRAZY. *(Holding her head, worse for the shouting.)* Oh, lordy. Fun doesn't pay.

(REGAN is heard chattering in the house. GONERIL enters, also with a large ice pack on her head, trailed by REGAN, who is combing her own hair and in fine spirits.)

REGAN. Oh, and the music and the dancing and the oboes and the ducks—
GONERIL. Swans.

51

REGAN. And the swans and the ducks and the violins and the caviar and the soup and all the footmen and handsome young people and old rich people and the gowns were cut so LOW and the codpieces were so BIG, HONEST TO GOD but that was FUN. And the Prince was so handsome and wonderful and everything was so CLEAN—Mother, it was CLEAN, I mean, I never imagined anything could be so CLEAN. It was all so CLEAN.

GONERIL. *(in some pain)* Keep it down, Regan. Mother had too much Royal punch.

MRS. SNOW. Where's Rosey? Tell that girl to get out here and bring some more ice. What's KEEPING that simpleton?

REGAN. *(Shouting in MRS. SNOW'S ear.)* ROSEY! MOTHER WANTS YOU! *(MRS. SNOW wobbles and collapses, holding her ears. GONERIL manages to keep her feet by clutching onto the porch.)* AND BRING SOME ICE! *(GONERIL collapses.)* Get up, Goneril, that's where the pig was sick. Oh, Mother, it was so NICE, it was really NICE, and the Prince danced with me, and the little man from the well danced with me—you should have danced, Goneril, I think you hurt the Prince's feelings when he kept asking you to dance and you just kept looking the other way and sucking your cheeks. And everybody was so pretty and that one beautiful, beautiful girl that came late and left early and smelled a little like pumpkin pie, oh, I've never in my life seen anybody so beautiful—

MRS. SNOW. Filthy slut, that's what she was. Who WAS that girl? It was all going fine until SHE got there.

ROSEY. *(Running out in her rags, disheveled.)* Sorry. I overslept. Sorry.

MRS. SNOW. Layabout. Good for nothing. Pick up my head. *(ROSEY puts MRS. SNOW'S head in her lap and applies ice.)* Who WAS that strange girl? That little trolly stole my thunder.

GONERIL. Trollop.

MRS. SNOW. Watch your language. Did you go to high school with that girl? Where did she get that coach? And that dress? And why did she run off like that at midnight? Something kind of skunky about that. Was that Dooley Sue Pookey? *(ROSEY realizes that MRS. SNOW is talking about her and nervously drops her head on the porch with a loud clunk.)* Watch out, you WOMBAT.

REGAN. No, Mother, Dooley Sue Pookey married an elf and moved to the veldt.

MRS. SNOW. She looked like Dooley Sue Pookey. Same beady eyes.

REGAN. She didn't have beady eyes. She looked a little like Rosey.

MRS. SNOW. OHO. HAH. Fiddlestick. That's what I say to that. Fiddlestick. That girl at the ball was CLEAN, Regan. I mean, she was really CLEAN. Not like Rosey. Rosey's a filthy mess. Aren't you, sweetheart? Don't look one bit like her. Looked like Dooley Sue Pookey.

GONERIL. Mother, it wasn't Dooley Sue Pookey.

MRS. SNOW. Well then who was it, Miss Smart Pants?

(MR. SNOW emerges from the house, still in long underwear.)

MR. SNOW. Where's my pants? What happened to my

pants? Who is it that can tell me where's my pants?

GONERIL. We've got to chip in and buy this man some pants.

ROSEY. You've got them right there in your hand, Father.

MR. SNOW. No I don't. *(He looks at the pants in his hand.)* Yes I do.

MRS. SNOW. I'm going to take a peek at your high school year book and see if I can't find that girl's face. I've seen that face someplace, I just know it. Rosey, go wash the goat. *(She stomps into the house.)*

REGAN. Mother, you let my yearbook alone. There's private personal messages written in there. MUTH-THUR. *(She follows her in.)*

GONERIL. Oh, give her a break, Mother.

MRS. SNOW. *(shouting from off)* I'll give her a break. You just be quiet and mind your sass.

GONERIL. *(Disappearing into the house with them.)* Mind your own sass.

MR. SNOW. *(following them in)* Now listen here, don't let's fight. Why don't we all just go back to bed and cuddle right up? Okay?

(ROSEY, left alone, sits down on the porch and sighs. ZED'S head appears from the hog trough.)

ZED. Hark. Silence.

ROSEY. Oh, hello.

ZED. How was the prom? Nice music?

ROSEY. Zed, it was wonderful. I danced so many times with the Prince. He danced with me more times than with anybody else. And he danced with Regan, too, and he asked Goneril several times but she just gnawed on her lip and stared at his codpiece and then she went off into the corner and drank seventeen Margaritas.

ZED. Nice girl.

ROSEY. Regan danced a whole lot with Mr. Troll, who's very sweet and makes bird call imitations when he's had too much to drink, and Stepmother drank a whole punch bowl and rolled under the table with the Queen's dog. They didn't even recognize me. And the King showed us how he could talk and burp at the same time.

ZED. Very chic.

ROSEY. Everybody was looking at me. They were all so rich. They had purple clothes and fat red jewels and all the women wore dead animals around their shoulders with eyes that looked back at you and made you feel odd for being so rich when they were so dead, only I wasn't rich, but I WAS, I think the Prince liked me a lot. It was wonderful.

ZED. Sounds like it.

ROSEY. What's the matter?

ZED. Nothing.

ROSEY. And just before midnight I realized I had to get home or I'd turn into a bowl of fruit or something, so I ran out and nearly killed myself on the lawn sprinkler and everybody ran after me but I was gone. Oh, Zed, I want so bad to be rich, you can't believe how wonderful it is, it's like a different world, so cultured and refined and sophisticated, and everybody's got diamonds and emeralds and rubies and they speak French and laugh at jokes

I don't understand and sniff things up their nose and the Prince looked like he stepped out of a painting or something, he knew what to do and he knew how to dance and he made me laugh and put me at ease and talked to me so gently and whirled me around, it was just like my dream, it was JUST like my dream, oh, I want to go back, I want to go back so bad—what's wrong?

ZED. I have to go.

ROSEY. You don't have to go.

ZED. Yes I do.

ROSEY. Where does the village idiot have to go? Stay here and talk to me.

ZED. You don't want to talk to me. I'm incoherent.

ROSEY. No you're not. As a matter of fact, you're talking better than I am this morning.

ZED. That's because you're talking bullshit.

ROSEY. Pardon?

ZED. I, on the other hand, am speaking in tongues and various Romance and non-Romance languages. Amo, amas, amat. Veni, vidi, vici. Ho perso il passaporto. Oú est la bibliothéque? Mein Freund Herbert und ich sind Studenten aus Amerika. La Vida Es Sueño. Futari no heya-ga hoshii desu. Kufungua kata hapa. Toy boat, toy boat, toy boat. Rubber baby buggy bumpers. She sells sea shells by the sea shore. The Leith police dismisseth us.

ROSEY. What happened to you? You're talking perfectly fine. You're talking so well, I don't know what the hell you're saying. *(What he has actually said, by the way, is, roughly, in Latin, Italian, French, German, Spanish, Japanese and Swahili, respectively, "I love, you love, he loves. I came, I saw, I*

conquered. I have lost my passport. Where is the library? My friend
Herbert and I are students from America. We want a double bed-
room. To open, slit here.")

ZED. I'm drunk. I'm thoroughly plotzed. I'm incoherent when sober, but I enunciate exquisitely when
snookered. Give up, don't care, talk fine. Thanks to
Mother Magee, and her wonder gin. I danced many dances
with Mother Magee. It was wonderful.

ROSEY. *(big discovery)* Zed, you're not an idiot.

ZED. Of course I'm an idiot. I live like an idiot, hole in
the woods, that's VERY idiot. Act like an idiot. *(He puts his*
finger to his mouth and burbles his lips.) BLABLABLABLA-
BLABLABLABLA. I belong to the village idiots union, I
go to the convention every year, I'd show you my mem-
bership card but I think I ate it. I eat like an idiot, berries,
leaves, grass. No chickens, though. Don't like that. Eyes
look up at you, little beady ones, say 'Don't wring my
neck, I've eggs to lay, poems to write, roads to cross,
SQUAWK!' So I just dress them up in little sweaters and
let them go. I look like an idiot, think like an idiot, walk
like an idiot, I think I must be an idiot, all the evidence
seems to point in that direction.

ROSEY. I don't understand. How did you get to BE like
this—I mean, how you are when you're not drunk—
when you—

ZED. Oh, I worked hard. Practice, practice, practice.
You can, too, if you want. Go to balls, hang around with
the upper classes.

ROSEY. Why would anybody want to practice to be
an idiot?

ZED. Because because because because BECAUSE.

Saw out the corners of things. Patterns, ghost stuff, just on the edge, little ghosty mechanisms, couldn't touch, nobody else could see, reach out, they run off. Different. Is bad. Maker of things. Not useful. Go on, go to the palace, devour small animals, make them into party hats. You'll be a big star.

ROSEY. You're not being very nice to me this morning. I thought you were nice.

ZED. You thought I was an idiot. Safe.

ROSEY. Well, what's wrong with being rich and living in a palace? Do you mind if I dream about it a little, when I'm not shovelling out the barn? I mean, is that a problem for you? My mother used to tell me such beautiful stories about—

ZED. Oh, God bless Mother. Bless her little heart. Pass the petunias.

ROSEY. She was a good mother.

ZED. Sure, for a three year old.

ROSEY. What does THAT mean?

ZED. Sorry. Drunk. It's my brain, you see. My brain gets to running in high gear and I can't stop it. And this affects my mouth, which begins to move, and prose comes out. Your mother was a saint. The Prince is a prince. Rich people are God's gift to the poor. Wallowing at their feet is a great privilege.

ROSEY. You're the one that made me go in the first place. I was scared to go and you taught me to dance.

ZED. That's what you wanted, wasn't it?

ROSEY. Yes. So what's your problem?

ZED. Oh, I haven't got any problems. What, me? The village idiot? Have any problems? No, far be it from me to try and explode your infantile delusions.

ROSEY. They're not delusions. Those rich people are REAL. They're not like us, they're REAL. And they SMELL good. And I've got a right to dream, I'm an oppressed person here, it's not easy being good all the time, you know, when your stepmother is a geek and your stepsisters are a freak show and your father can't find his pants—

ZED. You can handle them.

ROSEY. Who can?

ZED. You can run rings around those people every which way.

ROSEY. Then how come they push me around so much? Huh?

ZED. You let them.

ROSEY. No I don't.

ZED. Yes you do. Safe. *(He looks at her.)* Idiot. Jealous. Sorry. No brain. Sorry. *(He puts a finger to his head and pulls the trigger with his thumb.)* Bang. Sorry. Stupid. Nice ball, nice girl, very sorry, I gotta go now.

ROSEY. Wait a minute. Just wait a minute. You can't talk to me like that and then just walk away.

ZED. Yes I can. I'm an idiot. I can do anything I want. That's the beauty of it.

ROSEY. What are you trying to do? Make me feel as miserable as possible? Because if you're not, then please explain to me right now just what the hell you think you're talking about?

ZED. *(after a big sigh)* To dream of romance is natural. To hide conveniently behinds one's dream is neurotic. To worship the rich is cretinous. You don't remember your mother. You just remember remembering your mother. You hide behind the memory of this remembering in order to avoid the danger of having to experience any further growth, thus misunderstanding and subverting the whole purpose of the archetypal folk motif in the first place. Do you wish to have money? Why do you wish to have money? So you can give it away to other poor people? Then you will have no more money. Do you wish to marry a prince? Why do you wish to marry a prince? So you can act like a princess? How does a princess act? How, for example, does she urinate?

ROSEY. I think you're being terribly unfair. Many of those rich people are very nice. They can't help it if they're rich. They're just people, just like you and me.

ZED. Then why do you want to be rich?

ROSEY. Becuse it's better than this.

ZED. Why is it better than this?

ROSEY. Because this stinks.

ZED. Why does this stink?

ROSEY. Because everybody treats me like dirt.

ZED. I don't treat you like dirt.

ROSEY. You're treating me like dirt right now.

ZED. I'm treating you like an adult.

ROSEY. Well, stop it, I don't like it, this is a fairy tale.

ZED. The question is, what fairy tale is it?

ROSEY. It's MY fairy tale, so why do you keep butting into it?

ZED. I been trying to get the hell out of here all morning, but you keep calling me back to explain myself, then when you don't like what I say, you want me to go away again. Make up your mind, why don't you?

ROSEY. Zed, that palace is like a dream to me, I'm just striving here to throw off the shackles of my oppressors—

ZED. So you can turn into one. *(Pause. ROSEY stares at Zed. He stares back at her. Then—)*

MOTHER MAGEE. *(Singing, from in the well.)*
I LINED MY ASS
WITH BROKEN GLASS
AND CIRCUMCISED
THE SKIPPER.

ZED. Company.

(ROSEY and ZED look at each other. MOTHER MAGEE pops out of the well.)

MOTHER MAGEE. Hi, gang. How's tricks? Had a real nice ball, did you? Knew you would. Listen, you ain't seen nothin' yet. You just wait. I got a trick or two up my bloomers still. You just hold onto your nipples, girly. What's the matter here? You two look kinda constipated. What's the problem? Got gas? Feet sore? Don't all talk at once. Gonna be a big day today. I can feel it in my corns. Yes sir, there's a flutterin' in my wumpus. Could be a bat got in there. No, it's destiny, destiny closin' in on us, fate, karma, dramatic structure, the inevitable galloping kalump kalump towards the orgasm. I'm startin' to breathe hard. There's a tide in the affairs of fairy tale people, grab it when you can get it, don't let it pass you by. Can you feel the wind rushin', can you sense the little birds and rabbits leanin' over to see what happens, can you smell the fear, can you hear the trembling of the future beckon? God, I got myself so worked up, I'm gonna break wind.

(At this moment the loud sound of the PRINCE'S hunting horn booms out.)

MOTHER MAGEE. That's it! THAT'S IT! Here it comes. Big moment. Chin up, girl. Destiny. Destiny. I gotta lay off the pastafazoola. Come on, idiot, scoot, scoot. Go on, hog trough, hog trough, go. *(ZED looks at ROSEY, then goes and hides.)* Hang on, honey. Time for the climax. You're gonna like this, I promise. *(She is straightening ROSEY'S dress, putting her hair in place.)*

ROSEY. But what do I do?

MOTHER MAGEE. You just stand there and everything will come right to you. I gotta go. Wish I was you. Sure do. Stomach out. Chest in. Great. That's my girl. Smile now.

(She kisses ROSEY tenderly on the forehead and disappears into the well as the hunting horn sounds again, very close. For a moment ROSEY is alone, looking at her mother's grave.)

ROSEY. Help.

(TROLL appears.)

TROLL. OYEZ. OYEZ. HAIL AND FAREWELL. *(in a normal voice)* Hiya Rosey. How you been?

ROSEY. Fine.

TROLL. Good. Scuse me. *(once more bellowing)* PRINCE ALFRED OF FALFRED. FAFRID OF AFRID. WHAT-EVER. ALL RISE AND HAIL.

(He blows his tooter horn and sighs.)

TROLL. I hate this. I really wanted to be a shoe clerk.

(MRS. SNOW tugs GONERIL and REGAN out of the house, followed by MR. SNOW, still with his pants in his hand.)

MRS. SNOW. GOOD GOD, THE PRINCE. IT'S THE PRINCE. HE WANTS TO MARRY US. I JUST KNOW IT. Get out there, girls, and look clean. Don't pick your nose, Regan. Stand up straight.

(TROLL blows his tooter horn directly in MRS. SNOW'S ear. She collapses. Then he throws his obligatory confetti, which the PRINCE once again gets right in the face as he enters.)

PRINCE. *(wiping confetti away)* All right, Troll, thanks, puts the horn away, all right? Thank you. Now look, peo-ple, sorry to make a blather again, but—oh, hello there, Miss Snick, aren't you Goneril Snick? The one at the ball who sulked and talked to the cat? I've never seen any-body drink Margaritas like that.

MRS. SNOW. *(Stepping in to take over, horribly excited.)* Not Snick. Snook. I'm Mrs. Snock, and these are my granddaughters Gonoregan and Syphilis, Sisyphus.

Pegasus, Platypus. What IS your name, Regan?

REGAN. Regan.

MRS. SNOW. Thank you.

PRINCE. Well, yes. Good. I've got a slipper here, you see, and I need to find somebody who fits it. My beloved ran from the dance and left her shoe wedged in the lawn sprinkler, and whoever fits it gets a Prince. Me. The royal astrologers say so. Pointy hats, stars, moons, that sort. Also, Father says so, and the stars tend to go along with him, if they know what's good for them. Shoe. Show the shoe, Troll.

TROLL. *(showing the shoe)* Shoe. Shoe. Nice one, too.

MRS. SNOW. Oh, how exciting. Try MEEE. Try MEEE. Try MEEEEEEEEEE

GONERIL. Mother—

MRS. SNOW. TRY ME! TRY MEEE! TRYYY MEEEEEE! *(She is struggling to get one shoe off, falling over a lot, grabbing onto TROLL, the PRINCE, everyone, to keep her balance. She gives her shoe to the PRINCE, falls down, sticks her foot out.)* MEEEE. MEEEEEE. MEEEEEEE.

PRINCE. *(Looking at the shoe, and backing politely away from her foot.)* Well, if the woman wants it that badly, go ahead, Troll, although something tells me she's not the one.

TROLL. *(Skeptical, keeping his face as far from the foot as possible, trying the shoe.)* Errrrrrrrggggggggg. Uhhhhhhhhnn-ggggggggg. *(He and MRS. SNOW are having a terrible time, she is clutching and pushing at his head, he is grappling with her foot and legs.)*

MRS. SNOW. HARDER. HARDER. YES. YES. OH. OH.

TROLL. Errrrrrrfffffffff.

Mrs. Snow. HARDER, YOU PECKERHEAD.

Troll. This just isn't going to work.

Goneril. Mother, you're MARRIED.

Mrs. Snow. What's that got to do with the size of my feet?

Prince. I say, Troll, don't hurt yourself. Let's give Mrs. Snick's feet a breather and try the daughters, what?

Mrs. Snow. WAIT, Regan, go get the ax, we'll trim my feet.

Regan. Trim your feet?

Mrs. Snow. We'll just take a little off the heel, and a couple of toes, and it'll fit nicely.

Regan. Mother, YUK.

Mrs. Snow. Don't yuk your mother.

Troll. *(Moving towards GONERIL.)* Let's try this one, shall we?

Goneril. You stay away from my feet.

Troll. I just want to—

Goneril. You touch that foot and I'll bite your ear off.

Troll. Let's not over-react here.

Goneril. I won't have anybody messing with my feet.

Troll. I really think we should at least TRY—

Goneril. I don't feel good. Leave me alone. I'm ugly and everybody hates me and nobody loves me so everybody just back off and don't touch my feet.

Prince. I think you're lovely.

Goneril. Get lost.

Mrs. Snow. Don't tell the Prince to get lost. Give him your feet.

PRINCE. It's all right. She's a bit cranky today, is all. After the ball, and all. Anyway, I AM lost. I've always been lost.

TROLL. Maybe we can come back to her later. Let's try this one. You're—

REGAN. Regan. We danced a lot last night, remember? Then we went back into the pantry and played strip poker, and you had that incredible run of luck, and—

TROLL. *(Exchanging a nervous look with the PRINCE and cutting her off.)* YES, and it's a pretty little foot you have, indeed, isn't it?

REGAN. *(as he tries the shoe)* This is really a nice shoe. Do you have it in another color?

TROLL. Oh, what lovely feet you have. Oh, you have finely molded legs, too. And your lower and upper torso are rather nice, also. And I especially like your—

PRINCE. Let's not get carried away, Troll, all right?

TROLL. Yes sir. Sorry.

PRINCE. Doesn't fit, does it?

TROLL. No, not quite, no.

MRS. SNOW. I'll get the ax.

REGAN. Mother, NOOOOOO.

TROLL. No violence, please.

MRS. SNOW. *(Following REGAN around with the ax.)* It'll only hurt for a little while. You won't have to be on your feet much when you're a princess.

REGAN. MOTHER, STOP IT.

GONERIL. Put the ax down, Mother.

MRS. SNOW. Just a little bitty toe or two—we'll wrap your feet in tobacco leaves, pour on a little vodka, you'll never know the difference.

MR. SNOW. *(Picking his moment and deftly swiping the ax away from her.)* Let's hold off on the ax a bit, all right, dear?

MRS. SNOW. Delbert! You laid hands upon my ax. Get your hands off my ax.

TROLL. Well, I guess that leaves just YOU.

(He turns and points at ROSEY. Everybody turns and looks at her. Even MOTHER MAGEE and ZED stick their heads out to look. A moment of hushed silence.)

ROSEY. *(small voice, scared)* Me?

MRS. SNOW. Oh, no, is that really necessary? You don't want to put that nice clean shoe on any dirty-footed little cinderslut, do you? *(MOTHER MAGEE and ZED exchange a look and then disappear.)*

MR. SNOW. Now, you hadn't oughta talk that way, Gertie. She's my daughter, you know.

PRINCE. I think we should at least try her.

ROSEY. I don't know if I—

TROLL. Come on, sweetheart, let's just get it over with before your mother gets a hold of that damn ax again, all right?

ROSEY. But I don't know if I should. I mean, Goneril is the oldest.

GONERIL. That's right, say it. I'm an old maid. I'll always be an old maid. I've got cracks in my face and sags in my body and ice in my heart. Go on, insult me, torture me, bury me in sewage, I don't care. I don't care. *(She bursts into tears.)*

TROLL. Oh, dear. This just isn't working out like they

told me it would. Things are looking pretty grim.

(They all go over to comfort the sobbing GONERIL. ROSEY starts over, too, but MOTHER MAGEE reaches out of the well and pulls her back.)

MOTHER MAGEE. Go on, kid, this is it, it's now or never.

ROSEY. Well, I don't know, I mean—

(ZED sticks his head out from the hog trough.)

ZED. Go on. Put on the shoe. Don't listen to me. I'm drunk.

ROSEY. Yes, but—

MOTHER MAGEE. Come on, girl. Don't you want to be a princess?

MRS. SNOW. *(Looking around wildly.)* What the hell is all that stage whispering about?

MOTHER MAGEE. Uh oh. *(She pops back down the well. ZED is still looking at ROSEY. MRS. SNOW spots him.)*

MRS. SNOW. AHA! THERE'S AN IDIOT IN THE HOG TROUGH. JUST AS I SUSPECTED. JUST EXACTLY AS I SUSPECTED. JUST AS I EXACTLY SUSPECTED. STAGE WHISPERING IN THE HOG TROUGH. WHERE'S THAT AX? WHERE'S THE AX? GIMMEE MY AX BACK. *(She finds the ax and begins chasing ZED around with it.)* KILLLLL. KILLLLLLL. KILLLLLLLL.

REGAN. Daddy, do something. Mother's gone berserk. She's running amok. Mother's running amok.

MRS. SNOW. WAAAAHHHHHHHH! WAAAHHH!

KILLLLL! YAHHHHHHH! WAAAHHHHHHHH! *(A wild, maniacal chase around the yard ensues, MRS. SNOW chasing ZED with the ax and being chased in turn by MR. SNOW, TROLL, ROSEY and REGAN.)*

ROSEY. YOU LET HIM ALONE. STOP IT. STOP THAT. YOU MUSTN'T DO THAT. STOP IT.

REGAN. MURDER. MURDER.

TROLL. CITIZEN'S ARREST.

MR. SNOW. HEEL, GERTIE. HEEL. SIT.

PRINCE. *(Standing in the middle of all this as they run back and forth past him, trying to be the voice of reason.)* I say—. Pardon me. Hello? Isn't this a bit vulgar? *(ZED runs into GONERIL and falls over on top of her.)*

GONERIL. AHHHHHHHH. AHHHHHHHH. GET OFF ME. GET HIM OFFFFF ME. OOOOOOOOOO. COOTIES. AHHHHHHHHHHH.

MRS. SNOW. YAAAHHHHH. KILLLLL. YAAAHHH. *(MR. SNOW struggles with MRS. SNOW for the ax, and they tumble on top of ZED and GONERIL.)*

MR. SNOW. GIMMEEEE THAT AX, GERTIE, FOR CORN SAKE.

GONERIL. AAAHHHHHHHH. AHHHHH. AHHHH. *(ROSEY, REGAN and TROLL all pile one after another onto this now writhing, chaotic, screaming mass of arms and legs, trying to get the ax from MRS. SNOW.)*

MR. SNOW. YOU'RE GOIN' TOO FAR, NOW, GERTIE, NOW, GIMMEEE THAT THERE AX. *(He finally succeeds in wrestling the ax from her. ZED scrambles away from the mass of people.)*

MRS. SNOW. I'm shocked, Delbert. Delbert, I'm shocked. You've seized my ax, twice in one day. How dast you? How dast you? I'll rip out his throat with my **TEETH!** *(She lunges at ZED, growling and snarling like a dog. ZED runs out, dropping his little music mechanism unawares, as MR. SNOW tackles her and hold her down.)* **RRRRRRR. GRRRRRR. GOOD FOR NOTHING HOMELESS IDIOT TRASH. FILTH. MUGWUMP.**

MR. SNOW. *(On the ground with her, his hand firmly over her mouth.)* Now, calm down, Gertie, just calm down. Are you calm? *(She nods yes.)* Are you sure? *(She nods again. Cautiously, he takes his hand away from her mouth.)*

MRS. SNOW. *(Ostentatiously calm and serene, like the Queen serving tea.)* What's all the fuss about? I'm fine. I'm perfectly fine.

PRINCE. This is all moderately interesting, folks, but I really think we ought to get back to this shoe business, don't you? I'm supposed to have a wedding today, not some sort of primitive sacrifice.

MRS. SNOW. It was all that idiot's fault, your majesty. Some people just don't know how to behave in polite society.

ROSEY. He wasn't hurting anybody. Why can't you just leave him alone?

PRINCE. Look, Rosey, dear, if this idiot fellow distress you so, why don't I just have one of my archers ride out tomorrow and put the poor thing out of his misery, would you like that?

ROSEY. You mean kill him?

PRINCE. Well, he seems to upset you awfully much. *(The PRINCE is watching ROSEY'S reactions very carefully.)*

ROSEY. I'll try the shoe on. Just let him go, okay?

PRINCE. Oh, good. I like idiots myself. I feel especially

close to them. Lord knows, for the better part of my childhood, I WAS one, to hear Mother talk. Well, let's have a go at the shoe, what?

TROLL. You know, sir, I've got a feeling I've seen these feet before. These just might be the feet. These look to me like very promising feet.

REGAN. *(finding the dropped music thing)* He dropped something. What IS that? *(Everyone else is bent breathlessly over ROSEY, who has sat down by the well. TROLL prolongs the suspense by doing shoe clerk type things with the shoe.)*

PRINCE. *(sidling over to GONERIL)* Sorry about your feet and all. Are you all right? I can understand how you might be embarrassed about your feet, not that they're not feet, they're wonderful feet, I wouldn't mind having those feet myself, I just happened to notice ar the ball that you were so, well, stand-offish, and I've never quite come across that in a woman, being a Prince and all, but then, I do have a lot of trouble understanding people. Take your sister there, sitting by that well, just on the brink of princesshood, for all she knows, and I think I've never seen a sadder specimen in my life. What IS she thinking of? *(He looks up and sees that everyone is glaring at him for interrupting the breathtaking climatic moment of the putting of the shoe on ROSEY'S foot.)* Oh, sorry. Go right ahead. *(TROLL begins to go through his shoe clerk routine again.)* For God's sake, Troll, will you just stop futzing around and put the damn shoe on her foot.

TROLL. Righto.

PRINCE. Maybe you'd just as well do it yourself, dear, hmm?

ROSEY. All right. *(She takes the shoe.)*

PRINCE. Careful with it, though. *(The PRINCE looks at ROSEY. ROSEY looks at the PRINCE. REGAN is winding up the music thing.)*

MRS. SNOW. Put that thing down, Regan. You don't know where it's been.

REGAN. It plays music. Listen.

(The mechanism plays the waltz. For a moment they are distracted by the noise and look at REGAN. ROSEY looks at the shoe, hesitates, sighs then reaches over and drops it into the well.)

ROSEY. Oh, my, I've dropped the shoe in the well.

REGAN. *(Dropping the mechanism and pointing in horror.)* She dropped the shoe down the well.

(The music stops.)

MRS. SNOW. You did that on purpose. I saw you. Foul. FOUL. You did that because you KNEW Goneril's foot would fit and you didn't want her to have the Princess-ship. Cheater. OFF WITH HER HEAD. WHERE'S THE AX?

TROLL. Madam, control yourself, please. It was clearly an accident. Clearly. *(Aside, to ROSEY.)* Why did you DO that?

MRS. SNOW. I OBJECT. I DEMAND A RECOUNT. CALL IN THE MARINES.

REGAN. Oh, shut up, Mother.

MRS. SNOW. Shut up, Mother? SHUT UP, MOTHER? WHERE DID YOU LEARN MANNERS LIKE THAT? I'LL TEACH YOU TO SASS YOU OWN FLESH. I'LL

WRING YOUR GIZZARD, GIRL. I'LL FRY YOUR FISH. I'LL— *(GONERIL has taken the pants from MR. SNOW'S hands and now stuffs them into MRS. SNOW'S mouth.)* Urf. Ukkk. Erk.

MR. SNOW. Now, why didn't I think of that?

PRINCE. I hate to admit it, but the woman has a point. Miss Snick really didn't get a fair chance, did she? Suppose Goneril's feet had fit?

ROSEY. I'm sorry, Goneril.

TROLL. What are we going to tell the King? We can't go back without a Princess. I don't know what we're going to do. We could live in the woods and eat berries and fruit. Maybe I'll just go back down the well.

PRINCE. *(restraining him)* No, no, no.

ROSEY. I confess. I saw that it was just exactly Goneril's size, so I dropped the shoe in the well. She wins.

GONERIL. Rosey—

REGAN. It was a twelve wide?

PRINCE. All right. I'll accept that.

GONERIL. Now wait a minute.

PRINCE. I've rather a fancy for strong-minded brooders, you know. You remind me of my mother, actually, dear. Rather artistocratic. Took a fancy to you right off. I'll take you.

GONERIL. You want ME?

PRINCE. Well, uh, rather, I mean, uh, in a manner of speaking, yes. All right? Didn't it show?

GONERIL. I thought you were just making fun of me.

PRINCE. Oh, I wouldn't do that. I have no sense of humor whatsoever, do I, Troll?

TROLL. Not a bit.

GONERIL. You really want ME? Honestly?

PRINCE. I'm afraid so. *(GONERIL looks at him and then suddenly finds herself emitting a great booming, very silly and uncharacteristic stream of hysterical laughter.)* Well, I don't think it's all THAT funny.

REGAN. Look, Mother, Goneril's going to be a Princess. She's having hysterics. Isn't that exciting? Isn't that just the cat's meow? Speak up, Mother.

MRS. SNOW. *(Trying to pull the pants out of her mouth.)* Uffff. Urk. Ufff. Ufff. Erk.

MR. SNOW. She says yes. I think the buckle's wedged under her false teeth.

TROLL. *(Pulling on the PRINCE'S sleeve.)* Listen, uh, er—

PRINCE. What is it, Troll? Speak up.

TROLL. Could I have the other one?

PRINCE. I should think that's up to her, Troll, what? I mean, it's a free country. Well, not really, no, but still— You there, Hogan, do you want this Troll person here? You can have him if you like.

REGAN. Oh, well, uh, yes, maybe, no, yes. Yes.

PRINCE. And there we have it. Sorry there, Posey. Maybe next time. I hope you've learned your lesson about cheating and such.

ROSEY. Oh, yes.

MRS. SNOW. Uffffl. Urrrfluf. Eeeeee. Ooooo? Um?

PRINCE. Well, cheerio, we've got to be off, let's go, girls, you can send back for your things, if you have any things, we've got to go see the King and Queen now, what fun for you, poor kids. *(to ROSEY)* You're a lucky girl, you know, take my word for it. What I wouldn't give to be here in the woods picking flowers and such. *(He has taken ROSEY aside while the others congratulate GONERIL and REGAN.)* You're a nice girl, Rosey. And very perceptive. And a wonderful dancer. Thank you. *(He kisses her on the cheek. She opens her mouth to say something but he shushes her and immediately resumes his former tone.)* Ah, well, got to run, ta ta, bye bye, come along, folks.

REGAN. Goodbye, Rosey. Take care of Mother. *(She hugs ROSEY.)*

GONERIL. Goodbye, Rosey. Thank you. *(She hugs ROSEY, still giggling somewhat loonily.)*

MRS. SNOW. *(Jumping up and down and pointing to herself, pants still trailing from her mouth, one pantleg held by MR. SNOW to prevent her from wandering away, clearly indicating that she wants to come, too.)* EEEEEEEEEEE. EEEEEEE-EEEEEE. EEEEEEEEEEEE. EEEEEEEEEEEEEEE.

REGAN. Yes, Mother, we'll send you lots of dirty post cards. Oh, and wash the chickens, would you? Goodbye. *(They kiss MR. and MRS. SNOW and go off with TROLL and the PRINCE.)*

ROSEY. *(waving)* Goodbye. Goodbye.

MRS. SNOW. *(Finally getting the pants out of her mouth.)* They're gone. They've gone and left me. I'm a lone lorn creature. I'm abandoned. The parade's gone by. *(For a full moment she is a genuinely pathetic figure, standing there alone, clutching the pants, looking after them. Then, resuming her bitchy tone:)* There, Rosey, you see what you get for all you wickedness?

MR. SNOW. Gertie—

MRS. SNOW. Rosey has to stay at home and do the wash

while her sisters get to go off and serve the King and have slaves to help them empty the chamber pots and drink out of finger bowls and play croquet and eat raw oysters and what not. So there. Serves you right. Poetic justice. I always did say you were no good. You never WERE any good. I always said— *(MR. SNOW stuffs the pants back in her mouth.)* Urk. Uffflfl. Lek. Uffff.

MR. SNOW. Don't feel too bad, Rosey. Somethin'll turn up. Ripeness is all. That's what I heard, anyway. Come on, Gertie. Sit by the fire and cuddle. I like you this way. *(He takes one pantleg and leads her into the house.)*

MRS. SNOW. Urk. Urf. Ukkkk.

(They disappear. ROSEY is alone. She sighs once, then starts searching around on the ground near where REGAN dropped the music thing. MOTHER MAGEE appears from the well.)

MOTHER MAGEE. Well, you certainly blew that one, didn't you? What a klutz. You aren't supposed to drop the show down the well, dear. What's the matter with you? Don't you know the story? Look, I've got the shoe right here, run and find the Prince, maybe it's not too late. *(She pulls out what turns out to be the frog.)*

FROG. Brekkek.

MOTHER MAGEE. Oh, Christ. *(She starts to throw it back, gets an idea, gives it a big kiss, looks at it. Nothing happens.)* Another myth shattered. *(She throws it back in the well. Water splashes out.)* What are you lookin' for now, dearie? Drop a contact?

ROSEY. Here it is. *(She picks up the music mechanism.)*

MOTHER MAGEE. I swear, if I live to be thirty-seven, I'll

never understand you fairy tale people. Don't make no sense at all. What's that you're fiddlin' with there?

ROSEY. Nothing.

MOTHER MAGEE. Well, do what you please. You're a nice girl, but you're awfully weird. Excuse me. I've got to see a girl about a Prince. You're not the only one, you know. All kinds of storybook romance out there, just salivating for a fairy godmother. You take care now. I had high hopes for you. Looky there, it's the idiot.

(ZED appears, drinking from a flask.)

ZED. What happened? Where's the Prince? Get lost again? Here Prince. Here boy.

ROSEY. The Prince is marrying Goneril.

ZED. What for?

ROSEY. I don't know. He likes her.

ZED. Better than you?

ROSEY. I guess so.

ZED. The man's an idiot.

MOTHER MAGEE. You're talkin' pretty chipper for a half-wit, ain't you?

ZED. Won't last. I've got to stay drunk. Thanks for the stuff.

MOTHER MAGEE. What stuff? You mean the stuff in them little flasks I gave you? Why, that's nothing. Just a little ginger water. No alcohol in that. I don't drink.

ZED. But I can talk.

MOTHER MAGEE. Of course you can talk. And Rosey can dance. What do you think about THAT? HOW DO YOU LIKE *THEM* APPLES, HAH?

ZED. *(Looking at the flask.)* I don't understand. You told me—

MOTHER MAGEE. Yes, but I lied. Never touch the stuff. Rots your mind. Amazing thing, the mind. Make you believe a whole lot of crap about yourself, if you let it. Well, I got to run. See you in the funny papers. You just hoe your own row, cultivate your garden, don't mind me. Vamoose. Sayonara. Many happy returns of the day. Whatever the hell that means. *(She looks down the well.)* Judas Priest. That frickin amphibian just turned into a archduke. Stark naked and green as a cucumber. I don't believe it. Holy shit. TREAD WATER, HANDSOME, I'M COMING. GERONIMO. *(She falls head first into the well. Pause. There is no splash. ZED and ROSEY go over to look in, and immediately an enormous splash hits them both directly in the face.)*

ROSEY. *(Wiping water from her eyes.)* Oh, great. That's just great. The end to a perfect day. Here. You dropped your stupid music thing. I think it's broken. Perfect. *(She tosses the music thing to him.)*

ZED. Nawww. *(He fiddles with it.)*

ROSEY. It won't work, will it? It's broken, and it'll always be broken, and nobody can ever fix it.

ZED. I don't know. Hard to say. Could just be—

ROSEY. My Mother is dead and the Prince is gone forever and you're an idiot, even if you CAN talk without being drunk you're still an idiot and you're always going to be an idiot because you're POOR and you can't DO anything.

ZED. I do something. I make things.

ROSEY. You make things that break. What good is that?

I want to be a princess. I want to live in a castle and have fish eggs and marmalade for breakfast and wear nice dresses and be somebody and I just blew my whole entire life right there, Mother. You IDIOT. Why did you make me do that?

ZED. I didn't make you—

ROSEY. You did. You made me do it, and now my life is broken, everything is broken, somebody broke my palace and nobody can ever fix it again.

ZED. Sorry. *(He bangs the mechanism once sharply on his head. It begins to play.)* Here. You keep it. I got to go.

ROSEY. I don't want it. It's yours. You made it.

ZED. I can make another one. That's the beauty of it.

ROSEY. Oh. *(He starts to go, remembers, comes back to give her the music thing, starts to go again.)* You don't think maybe I just had the wrong fairy tale, do you? *(ZED looks at her, shrugs, starts away.)* Do you want to dance?

ZED. Who?

ROSEY. You.

ZED. Me?

ROSEY. Ya.

ZED. Uh. Sure.

(She puts the music thing down, takes a deep breath, and they begin to dance. Swirling lights. Fade to black.)

NOTES

The oldest extant written version of the Cinderella story dates from China in the 800's AD, but the story was no doubt by then already ancient. In the version recorded in Grimm, the representative of the dead mother is a bird that lives in a tree that grows from her grave, the stepsisters cut off parts of their feet so they can fit the slipper, and at Cinderella's wedding to the Prince, birds come and peck out the stepsisters' eyes. It is from Charles Perrault's later and more refined version that we get the fairy godmother, the pumpkin coach, the lizard footmen and such, and the bloody business with the ax is eliminated. But in many ways, Perrault's expurgated version misses the point—and does so, I think, on purpose. The Grimm version is a story told by poor people. The Perrault version was the product of an aristocratic society and was for rich people—it upheld the values of the aristocracy and minimized the darker aspects of poverty, presenting them as somehow deserved.

It is interesting that the most powerful version of the Cinderella story, Shakespeare's *King Lear,* which shifts the focus from the outcast daughter, Cordelia, to the highly problematic father, is in its own way a kind of revolutionary assault upon the hypocrisies and abuses of privilege. Cordelia is punished for telling the truth. Edgar is forced to impersonate a beggar to save his life, and in doing so discovers truths he had not suspected in his other state. And Lear, divesting himself of all the trappings of wealth and power, discovers on the heath the true horrors of the poor naked wretches he has ignored in his years of wealth and arrogance. The child is as much at the mercy of its parents as the citizen is at the mercy of the state, and the poor at the mercy of the rich. The fairy tale allows the child to deal with her resentment and frustration at the basic unfairness of this situation, as in some respects art and ceremony allow the poor to experience vicariously the imagined pleasures of the rich.

Zed is at the bottom of this world, as Prince Alf is at the top, but both are to some extent victims of the social and economic structure they have been born into, and both have a chance, ultimately, and within certain limits, to exercise a certain amount of choice in their lives, as does Rosey, who is at the beginning of the play only a little ways above Zed in the social heirarchy, but has the opportunity, through the intervention of Mother Magee, to rise up to the topmost level, a place she believes she has always wanted to be. The happiest of the three sisters is Regan, who tends to live completely in the present moment, has only the vaguest sense of future consequences, and is not tortured by the past. Goneril is suspicious and resentful of all opportunities to escape from her unhappiness. She hides in it, wrapping it around herself like a blanket. And Rosey has been living in a fantasy world—protecting herself from the unpleasantness of her situation by imagining an impossibly beautiful other world inhabited by the rich, a world very unlike the one that Prince Alf actually lives in, with his harridan mother and tyrant father.

Rosey associates this impossible vision of wealth and high position with the memory of her mother, but when her surrogate mother appears from the well in the form of Mother Magee, she turns out to be not at all what Rosey imagined—she appears to be coarse, scatter-brained, lusty, wildly eccentric and rather a mess, and her ticket to the ball may in fact turn out to be a ticket to somewhere else entirely. In a fairy tale, as in a play, there is first a situation with some potential for arousal (Rosey is unhappy and wants to change her life, but doesn't know how, and so escapes into a world of fantasy) which is pierced suddenly by some unexpected event (the fantasy begins, amazingly, to come to life—there is a troll in the well, and he is handing out invitations to the ball)—which precipitates a crisis caused by the sudden intense arousal of hope (are there tickets for them? will there be enough tickets for everybody? who will be saved?)—which turns to the possibility of unexpected joy as Prince Alf, the living embodiment of Rosey's dreams, appears and does give them the tickets, this hope only to be shattered by another, more serious obstacle, that is, that Mrs. Snow is going in Rosey's place, plunging the heroine into a new and deeper despair as the hope held out is taken away again, which state of affairs is broken again when someone else appears from the well, the fairy godmother, who offers her own kind of ticket, fraught with difficulties and embarrassment, but with the promise of turning all humiliations into lasting joy, even as the lizards will be turned to footmen by the magic of the word *novotny.*

But this is not enough, even, because Rosey raises

further objections—she can't dance, and Mother Magee is suddenly gone. The neurotic, says Freud, when presented with the object of her desires, runs from it in terror, has learned to love despair, has become comfortable in the safe illusion of her particular neurosis, her pain is a comfort to her, the role of victim is safe. She is in reality perfectly capable of dancing, as she finds out later—she knew how all along, but she hid that knowledge from herself out of her fear of actually being in a position to act in such a way as to make her fantasies come true—that is, her fear of having some choice, and therefore some responsibility, in the matter, and in the course her life will take.

And the ball is in fact, on the surface, at least, pretty much everything Rosey had imagined it would be. It all happens more or less as the fantasy had been played out countless times in her imagination. But then, just when the fairy tale is about to move itself to its logical and inevitable conclusion, Zed appears to spoil it for her—because taking action, taking the risk, has allowed her mind to expand a bit, enough to begin to be able to see the world in Zed's way, and it looks very different from his point of view. To become one of the rich and powerful is not exactly what she had thought it would be, after all. The basic problem and hidden nightmare at the core of every form of success is that, having struggled against nearly impossible odds to reach a certain state, one finds oneself, once one has arrived there, turning step by step into a person very much like one's former enemies, the people who had tried hardest to stop one from achieving that success. The price one pays for conquering one's enemies is that one often turns into them.

The child, trapped in the world of large and powerful adults, wants desperately to be grown up, so she can be as powerful as those who now control and often oppress her—but when the child does grow up, she discovers that adults had only appeared to be strong because she was so weak—the adult in fact feels like a child still, and tries to hide this, because she still presumes that all the other adults are really adults, and are not really still children, like her. In a like manner the poor and oppressed struggle and defeat the rich and powerful, and then turn into them and become bigots and oppressors themselves, as the parent often finds herself saying and doing to her children exactly the same things that infuriated her when she was a child. To some extent this cycle of regeneration is as inevitable as getting old and moving towards death—but there is also some possibility, within the framework of this archetypal inevitability, of achieving, with some effort, a certain amount of apparent freedom and maturity, and that, in a simplified way, is what many fairy tales are actually about. And as the child grows older, the fairy tales seem to grow more complex, because the child grows capable of perceiving more ambiguity in a situation that at first seemed very simple and clear. It is in part this ability to discover the ambiguity behind the structure of the fairy tale that indicates genuine growth and a movement toward maturity. It is a characteristic shared by fanatics of all persuasions, religious and political, that they cannot tolerate ambiguity—either they simply can't see it, or they see it but refuse to acknowledge its importance, considering the ability to perceive levels of ambiguity and a complexity of motives as characteristic of weak persons who can take no action because they see too many sides of every issue.

This logic that hates and rejects ambiguity is the voice of the child in us, an ancient animal voice that all oppressors have used to reduce us to the state of children again so they can control us. But these self-appointed adjudicators are not the metaphysical adults they pretend to be. They are more like the playground bully who is himself a child, just a bigger and stronger child with contempt for the smaller children who can often read and think and feel complex things the bully is either incapable of feeling or is too frightened to admit he feels. Propaganda is a kind of ill-conceived, bastard fairy tale through which such bullies can lead entire nations to think and act like demented children. In the theatre, this role of oppressor and ogre is often assumed by the reviewer, who eschews investigation in favor of instant judgement, a kind of schizophrenic fluctuation between worship and assassination, often reflecting the reviewer's deep feeling of ambivalence towards those who do what the reviewer in most cases either cannot, is afraid to, or has chosen not to do—that is, summon up the courage required to actually create something.

In this play, Rosey is given a choice—to accept the role the traditional fairy tale assigns to her, and thus to act as any respectable fairy tale heroine is expected to act, and to fulfill her childhood fantasy and become a Princess, or to make a much darker and, to the other children in her world, perfectly insane choice, to investigate the more ambiguous and dangerous world represented by Zed, who spends his time not, like the Prince, killing small animals for amusement, but rather in making little mechanisms that generate beauty and joy and cause people to come together in that complex ritual of shared movement and intimacy, the waltz. What began as a Cinderella story turns out to have been all along acutally a version of "Beauty and the Beast." The playwright is the idiot. The play is the mechanism. The performace is the dance.

A NOTE ON THE MUSIC

The best way to get the music box effect is probably to put someone just offstage with a good view of what's going on and have them play the music box tune whenever appropriate on a small xylophone or other instrument capable of making the delicate sound a music box makes. Recording the sound is a much less satisfactory solution.

The only other music in the script—Rosey's fantasy of the ball in the first scene, should be the eeriest possible recording of the main theme of Johann Strauss's 'Vienna Blood.' (*Wiener Blut,* Op. 354).

DOLORES WALTZ

E. WALDTEUFEL